The Edge of Nothingness

Shayne Carmichael

At the age of ten, Zach witnessed the death of his mother and the kidnapping of his sister during a vampire raid on their village. For years, the memory of that night and the face of the vampire who saved him from certain death have haunted him. Talked into the insanity of a resistance-backed raid on vampire territory, Zach comes face to face with the vampire he couldn't forget.

(This title was previously published but has been revised.)

Arian Derwydd Books, LLC

https://arianderwyddbooks.com/

The Edge of Nothingness

Chapter 1

Craning his head slightly, Zach could see his sister down below him, searching for him. He'd found the perfect hiding place on the roof of the old storehouse. From here he could see almost the entire village. The sun burned low in the sky, and the warmth of it heated the air. From his vantage point, Zach had a good view of the placid ribbon of the Plat River as it wound its way north of the village. The stream picked up current as it flowed east toward the falls, then became a white rush of water spilling over the black rocks at the fall.

Kat had already tried to find him in the building but hadn't looked on the roof. Probably because both of them knew their mother would have a fit. She disappeared into the woods but then returned a few moments later.

"Zachary Bern, you come out now!" His sister demanded as she stomped her foot. When only silence greeted her command, she huffed off, yelling, "I'm going to tell mom!"

The sun had already begun its descent beneath the horizon, and Zach really didn't want to give up his spot yet. Resting his chin on his hands, he watched the sky darken to twilight, and the twinkling light of the stars grew stronger as the sun finally disappeared completely. It felt peaceful to Zach, but he knew that wouldn't last long when his sister came back.

Even though he was older than Kat by four

years, most times he didn't mind when she bossed him around. She was only six and generally he let her tag along with him. When Kat came back, dragging their mother by the hand down the lane, he sighed. Time to give up his perfect hiding spot. As they stopped in front of the building, his mother called out, "Zachary, get out here now. It's way past time for dinner."

Before Zach could stand, several dark figures came out of the nearby woods. As he started to rise to shout out a warning, the swift, unexpected movements of the other people stunned him. They moved incredibly fast. When one of them grabbed his mother, Zach froze with the high-pitched terror of her scream. Even more cloaked figures swarmed from the trees, heading in the direction of the village. In the bright silver glow of the moon, he could see the fear on his mother and sister's faces.

Still Zach couldn't force his limbs to move. He lay plastered to the roof, helpless as a man held his mother pinned to him with one arm. The other wrapped around his sister's wrist, seeming unperturbed by their struggles. Beneath his arm, suspended against his side, Kat wriggled desperately to free herself.

In front of his eyes, the man buried his face against his mother's throat as she screamed and tried to kick her way free. Zach could feel nothing but horror as he realized the dark figure was a vampire. His mother's struggles weakened, and her scream faded into silence. Immobile beneath his own fear, there was nothing Zach could do. Disbelief rose with the terror; this couldn't possibly be happening.

In the distance, he heard more screams and shouts from the direction of the village. When the vampire dropped his mother's body, her sightless eyes stared up into the sky and tears blinded Zach.

Kat's terrified sobs went unabated as another figure approached from the woods. "Hel, if you're going to keep that one, shut her up. Reto will be here soon. He wants to bed down for the day then return to Forest Crest."

They both ignored the dead body laying in the dirt near them. When he pulled back his hood, Zach saw the arrogant lines of the man's features.

"Since when have I listened to Reto."

Zach memorized each detail of his mother's murderer. Ungodly beautiful in the way of vampires, blonde hair spilled around his shoulders, framing the pale, sweetly curved visage. He seemed like an angel come to life, but the blood on his lips gave lie to the false innocence. Beyond scared, Kat did no more than whimper against the hold on her.

"Don't push your luck, Hel. You run the Blood Assara by his grace." With a sneer, he added, "Or are you ready to take Reto on?"

Hel's features distorted into pure anger, twisting the handsome face. "Shut up, Vel. Just shut up."

"Take only the young ones, the rest we feast on. Those are his orders." Vel didn't bother to hide his smirk of amusement.

From the direction of the village, a fire began to burn against the night sky. Zach could hear screams and shouting and caught glimpses of running people through the trees as they tried to escape.

Several vampires came from the village, leading a roped line of prisoners down the lane toward the old storehouse. When they stopped in front of the building, Hel strode over to the humans and picked the end of the rope, tying it around Kat's neck. After dropping her to the ground, he went inside. Two of the vampires walked along the line and untied three of the mortals. Their victims struggled violently as they were dragged into the building. A few vampires remained outside to guard the humans as the others followed Hel. Though the night was warm, Zach shivered uncontrollably as he tried not to sob.

Long draw screams, shrill in their intensity, battering Zach's ears. He didn't want to know what was happening, and he covered his ears to try to block it out. Occasionally a vampire would walk out of the building, toss a body carelessly to the ground before grabbing another and going back in.

The carnage of torn victims, their organs spilling from the dead shells of their bodies, scented the air with their blood. Zach saw the face of his teacher, twisted in the agony of her death. A hole had been torn out of her chest, the mass of her insides exposed from her throat to her stomach. Swallowing thickly against the rise of bile in his throat, Zach closed his eyes tightly to block the sight, but it didn't help. The screams still battered relentlessly in Zach's ears.

Several vampires came out into the open yard, and one began walking down the lines of prisoners. As she pointed to a human, another vampire stepped forward and unknotted the rope around her neck. The young girl sobbed piteously but the female vampire grabbed her wrist and yanked her forward. A third vampire coiled another rope around the girl's neck then waited for the next chosen prisoner. As each was pulled forward, the rope was looped and tied around their throats. When the vampire approached Zach's sister, he almost cried out in protest, then bit his lip so hard it started to bleed. Only the young were taken and once finished, four of the vampires began leading the humans toward the woods.

Zach felt the despair of being unable to do anything. It blackened his soul and tears spilled down his cheeks as he shriveled inside himself. Resting his forehead to his arm, his body shook with the sobs he tried to suppress.

An eternity later, there were no more vampires or people coming from the village. Zach wasn't sure if any had escaped or not. He could only pray his father and brother had gotten away. He hadn't seen them in any of roped prisoners that huddled despairingly in the yard.

Screams continued to erupt sporadically from inside the storehouse and didn't fade until long moments later, sometimes abruptly cut off in mid-sound. Zach didn't dare move at all. He knew he had to stay where he was until the sun rose. Then he could get out of there and try to find his sister.

Several dark shapes appeared soundlessly behind the four vampires guarding the prisoners. Sudden flashes of metal glinted in the moon light before the stakes were thrust into the unsuspecting backs. Without a sound, the bodies crumpled and several more figures appeared out of nowhere. The tallest figure pulled out a sword and the others followed. With efficient speed they sliced the heads of the vampires from their bodies.

For some reason, none of the prisoners made any noise and when Zach glanced over at them, he saw every last one of them appeared to be in a daze. As the cloaked figures pulled back their hoods, Zach knew in an instant they were vampires as well. An unearthly glow to their skin betrayed what they were.

With one motion from the man in the center, the rest spread out to block the exits of the building. Long, black hair lay in thick waves around a pale, set expression. Zach thought there was disgust etched in the lines, but a moment later there was nothing but blankness to the man's features. Forcing himself to brand the face into his mind, Zach swore someday he would kill them all.

When one of the doors opened, the man lifted his hand. A horrible shriek followed, and a second later a vampire on fire lurched into the yard below. Zach smelt the unmistakable odor of burning flesh. The shouts of the other vampires in the building erupted as the vampire collapsed to his knees and fell face first to the ground. As they poured out of the doors, they were met in fierce battle by the vampires waiting outside.

Everywhere Zach looked, bodies were engaged in bloody combat. The gleam of swords and stakes repeatedly flashed in the glow of the moon. Seriously outnumbered, the first group of vampires fell fairly quickly.

"Jai, gather the bodies and stack them in the building, then torch it!" The black-haired man yelled out as he fought with Hel. They had both stripped out of their cloaks and wore only pants and boots.

"Yes, Night!" The man yelled back before he motioned to several of the others. They began dragging the fallen vampires across the ground and in the storehouse.

Grim determination settled on the faces of Night and Hel as their swords clashed with deafening sound. They circled each other, trying to find an opening in their opponent's defense. Hel's body bore many bloody marks, but Night's had only one, where the tip of Hel's sword had caught him on the arm.

Zach saw something oddly beautiful in the deft movement of limbs as Night pressed his attack on Hel, forcing the other vampire back. He had heard tales of them, but he'd never seen a vampire, since none had ever come to his village in his short lifetime. They lived across the border where the rivers of blood red waters flowed.

In a lightening blur of motion, Night parried a blow meant to cleave through his arm. Before Hel could bring his sword back around, Night brought his down on Hel's head with all his strength. The blow sliced through the skin and bone of Hel's head and throat. It didn't stop until the blade stuck from the vampire's neck. With a harsh growl, Night forced the sword free, and Hel dropped to the ground.

He was so engrossed in the battle below, Zach didn't notice the flames licking up the side of the building. The smoke alerted him to the danger of his position, and Zach frantically jumped up and turned to get back to the small hatchway.

An arm wrapped around him, and he felt himself lifted into the air. Too frightened to struggle, Zach's heart raced with the empty space between him and the ground. His fingers clung desperately to the arm around him, finding the flesh hot to the touch.

"I've got you." A soft voice spoke near his ear, but nothing stilled the panic inside Zach. Already the spot where he had been was engulfed in flames. The bright glow and acrid smell of the fire singed his senses.

A moment later, Zach felt solid ground beneath his feet and the arm released him. Whirling around, he found himself face to face with the vampire, Night. Fathomless blue eyes stared into his and Zach stumbled back, trying to get away. Something in the depths of those eyes fascinated and frightened him. The vampire's face, too close to his own, appeared smooth, ageless, unflawed. Zach could still feel the heat of that skin on his fingertips.

As Night took a step toward him, Zach flailed wildly out with his fists. Taking another step back, the heel of his shoe caught on a rock, and he tumbled backward. Bright stars burst across his vision as sudden pain shot through his head, then blackness descended.

Chapter 2

Zach's eyes flew open. The dream still painfully fresh in his mind, even with the cool autumn breeze coming through the open window above his bed. Ten years had passed since that night, yet every detail remained vivid, replaying over and over. Wiping his hands down his face, he sat up slowly, stretching and rolling his shoulders to get the kinks out.

"Zach?" Harriet Laden poked her head in his bedroom door. "Oh, you're up already. Markus needs you in the south field."

"I'll be there in a minute, just need to get dressed."

He waited until his foster mother left before standing. The threadbare blanket fell to the floor and Zach tossed it onto the bed. He dressed quickly, opting for his less-than-pristine work pants and work boots. After slipping on a stained white tunic, he stared for a moment at the sword leaning against the wall by his bed. Chances were, he wouldn't need it, and he had to still the urge to keep from picking it up. Opting instead for his hunting knife, he slid the weapon into the shorter scabbard of his belt and buckled the belt around his waist.

As he stepped out into the bright sun, he shielded his eyes, scanning the field for Markus. Spotting the gray and black hair, he started for the man, readying himself for another day's work.

Markus grunted and waved toward the wagon

without looking at him. "Morning, son. Fetch me the water can, will you?"

Zach handed the water can down to Markus and for the next five hours, they went through the field, tending to the less hearty crops. By the time they were done, Zach's stomach rumbled loud enough to wake the dead. Markus finally called a halt to the work, wiped his brow with his rumpled hat, and tossed the tools and water can back into the wagon.

"How's the fight going?" Markus asked as they headed back toward the small farmhouse.

Zach pulled the wagon effortlessly along, blinking the sweat from his eyes. "It's going well. Brant Conner is hell bent on pushing our advantage, though."

Markus growled a little. "That boy's nothin' but trouble. Mark my words: Brant Conner will wind up like his brother, drained and dumped into the woods."

"I know. He's… reckless."

"He's dangerous," Markus said gruffly. "Dangerous and with just enough money to do whatever he pleases, even to the detriment of those around him."

"I'll keep my head about me. Don't worry, Markus." Zach smiled over at the man who'd become a father figure to him since his own father had gone missing.

Markus stopped walking and nodded. Eyes that showed a soul far older than the body it inhabited stared up at Zach. "You do that, son. You might not be ours by birth, but we love you just the same. Would tear my Harriet up if somethin' happened to you." Markus tilted his head in the direction of the house. "Come on now. She's waitin'."

The aroma of fresh-baked bread drew them into the house and Zach breathed it in deep. Harriet buzzed around in the small kitchen, dingy white apron tied around her waist as she flit from one place to another. The woman was unstoppable. Markus just laughed and shook his head, leaving his dirt-encrusted boots at the door. Zach set his boots beside Markus' and followed him into the kitchen.

Lunch was relaxing and when he finished, Zach excused himself. He had matters to attend, and while Markus supported the resistance, Harriet did not allow discussion of such sort anywhere in her house. She was adamant about her men staying out of it. Zach, however, couldn't do that. He'd seen the horrors vampires could inflict on humans, and he refused to rest until every damn one of them was destroyed.

"We cannot sit idly by and wait for them to destroy us!"

Zach groaned when he heard Brant Conner's voice thundering from the tavern. No doubt the man was stirring up more, unneeded fervor. Sighing, Zach opened the door and stepped in. Only a few heads turned to acknowledge him; everyone else was too busy listening intently to Brant's fire-fueled preaching. The man was a menace, a dangerous spark in the powder keg of the resistance movement. Ordering a mug of ale from the barkeep, Zach kept his distance, schooling his features into something less scowling.

"He's been at it all day."

Zach just nodded and took a swallow of ale, giving Joseph Durrand a glance out of the corner of his eye. "He's trouble."

Joseph sighed and looked over at the steadily growing crowd surrounding the table on which Brant stood. "That he is. But aside from you, he's the strongest we've got."

Zach wanted to dispute that, but he kept his mouth shut, opening only to drink. Brant Conner might be strong, but it was in physical brute strength only. The man had the common sense of a pebble.

"But what about the treaty?" someone piped in.

"Treaty? You call that a treaty?" Brant shouted. He waved his hands madly about, grand sweeping gestures to make his words sound as powerful as he seemed to think they were. "Humans are under servitude to the vampires! We owe them nothing, yet we serve them!"

Zach had enough. Tossing back the last of his ale, he went over to the crowd and muscled his way through it until he was face to face with Brant. "Have you not learned anything?"

Brant sneered at him. "Well, well… if it isn't Zach Bern. And where have you been while the rest of us have been working diligently for our freedom?"

"Our freedom?" Zach crossed his arms over his chest and glared. "What you are proposing is nothing more than walking in and turning your soul over to them. If you raid the vampires' lands, you will all die!"

"Then we die fighting!"

A chorus of cheers met his pronouncement, every one of the fools siding with Brant. Zach walked away, body tight with tension. He dropped into the nearest chair with a huff, eyes locked onto Brant as the man slapped hands with several men in the crowd. They were walking straight for death, that much was certain. This was one fight Zach absolutely refused to go along with.

That was… until Kurt Laden came into view. He was Zach's foster brother, the only child of Harriet and Markus Laden. Like the others, Kurt cheered Brant Conner on, hell bent on destruction on a grand scale. Ice formed a knot in Zach's stomach when he realized Kurt was part of this. It, in essence, sealed Zach's fate.

The crowd thankfully died down after another fifteen minutes, Brant ordering everyone a round. As several others hung around to speak with Brant, Kurt made his way to Zach and Joseph.

"Gods, what a speech!" Kurt sat in the chair across from Zach.

"Mm, what a speech," Zach echoed with disdain. "Please tell me you aren't seriously considering joining him."

Kurt looked taken aback. "Well, of course, I am! I have a duty to protect my people, my family." He pointed a finger at Zach. "And so do you, Zach. How can you sit around and watch everyone give themselves so freely to preserve our lives? Especially after what you went through."

Gritting his teeth, Zach reigned in his temper in record time. "Brant Conner is nothing but a war-hungry, hot-headed boy who has no semblance of common sense."

"He's strong," Kurt countered bitterly. "So are you. We need you, Zach."

"Nothing you say is going to make me join in this insanity."

"I need you."

Except that.

Zach studied his brother, finally coming to the realization that he simply could not let Kurt go alone. "I'll have your hide for this."

"Take it out on the vampires," Kurt said with a triumphant smirk.

* * *

The sun had long set by the time Zach collapsed onto his bed. The meeting had gone just as he'd figured: downhill. Brant Conner was sure to get them all killed, but with Kurt determined to fight, Zach had no choice but to go with them. Sighing, Zach stretched out, muscles pulling tight. He felt too wound up to sleep, too much on his mind. He couldn't tell Harriet and Markus about Kurt; it would devastate them. Glancing over at his sword, Zach said a silent prayer to the gods that they made it home safely, even if it wasn't likely.

He rolled onto his stomach and shifted

restlessly. Sleep eluded him, though a part of him was grateful for that. The nightmares haunted him relentlessly, night after night. And gods… the face that was burned into his memories tormented him. Eyes as blue as the darkest depths of the sea stared back at him, intense and terrifying. Zach squeezed his eyes shut, praying it would block the visions.

Forcing himself to think of something better, he conjured up images of Luci Brackett, the daughter of the village blacksmith. Luci was a beautiful young woman—full of life and laughter. Her golden hair fell in long curls over her shoulders, and when she smiled, the corners of her mouth drew up in a sweet smile. The images of vampires faded, leaving Zach with thoughts of curves and smooth, creamy skin.

He began to harden and rocked his hips slightly, the friction exquisite against the blanket. Lifting his hips, he pushed a hand beneath him, biting into the pillow to stifle the groans as he thrust into the tunnel of his fist. Luci's lips taunted him as she laughed, her breasts full and inviting. He rolled in his bed, strokes quickening. His heart pounded away, his breath becoming labored. Luci slipped to her knees, mouth open and waiting. Then she looked up.

Zach screamed into the pillow as he came, his seed coating his hand as blue-black eyes stared down at him from the face of a vampire. Shaking and breathless, Zach collapsed, body jerking with the last of his tremors. Sleep set in quickly, bringing with it unwanted dreams of those damned eyes.

Dawn brought no relief. Zach found himself standing with the others while they all waited for Brant to emerge from his family's house. When Brant did come out, the cheers were deafening. Yet, true to his word, Zach stayed at Kurt's side. Sword at the ready on his left hip, he marched on when the others did. Straight on to their deaths.

* * *

In a very short time, their band of men had gone from jubilant to complete chaos. All around Zach, the others had been quickly disarmed by the troop of vampires who had descended on them from out of nowhere. Out of the corner of his eye, he saw Brandt and his brother still fighting furiously.

Though the vampires seemed oddly disinclined to injure them, Zach had no such compunction. His sword viciously slashed through the air each time one tried to get near him. He'd already caught two of the vampires off guard, but when he sought to press his advantage, they'd back off. It was the strangest battle he'd ever been in.

Brandt shouted and cursed as he fought the vampires off. Suddenly one of them got too close to Brandt, and he was forced to jump back to avoid the edge of the sword. Brandt grabbed Kurt's arm and shoved the young man in front of him, using him as a shield.

"You fucking coward!" Rage erupted in Zach as he rushed them, knocking Kurt out of the way. Faced with the enraged Zach, Brandt had to fight off the stunning blows of Zach's sword as Zach tried to kill him.

"I'm going to fucking kill you!" Zach screamed at him as he drove Brandt backward. The clang of their swords echoed between the trees.

"We better stop them, before they kill each other. You take him, I'll get the other." One of the vampires brought up his staff and landed a hard blow to the side of Zach's head. Before Brandt could react, the same action from another vampire brought him down as well.

Chapter 3

Leaning, palms flat, against the stone of the parapet, Night gazed out at the rolling landscape of his domain. Though his elder had entreated him several times to live in the capitol, Night had refused. Nothing could compare with the silver glow bathing his land in the warmth of its light.

He'd found contentment in the earth that supported him, feeling the strength of it coursing through him constantly. If he strayed too far from it for long, it would fade from him. As the strongest of the border Dominions, he held the largest domain, bordering the land of the human settlements. A border he had always vehemently protected and would continue to do so.

"Night?" She spoke quietly as she approached him from behind.

When he turned to face her, he saw she carried a goblet with her. Resting back against the stone, he held out his hand for it. The willow-slim, young lady was a far different creature than the one he had brought to his home years ago.

"I thought you would be hungry. You didn't feed after you read the letter from your elder."

"You keep too good of an eye on me."

"I know when you are troubled, Night. You've always sought solace up here when something bothers you."

"This time Tere tells me it is very important for

me to travel to the Peak." Something he really had no interest in doing. It would take him farther from his home than he wanted to be.

"I've heard things. From Orshan's mortals. They are so badly treated. Too many of them are sickening and dying because they aren't given enough food. The new master Orshan hired is far worse than the last one he had."

Night could see it in her eyes. She looked to him to do something about it. "Tell the cook to open the kitchen to them, Kat. And let them know they will find a meal here if they need."

She hugged him tightly, almost throwing him off balance. "Can I tell Orpheus to prepare some medicines?"

"Yes, you may."

She squealed in an unladylike fashion as she lifted her face to his. "Thank you, Night. Thank you so much." She punctuated the words with several kisses to his cheek.

Twining one of her dark curls around his finger, he tugged at it playfully. "You have me wrapped around your little finger, sweetheart. Now go talk to cook and Orpheus like I know you want to do."

She released him then turned with a small bounce in her step and headed back into the house. It seemed a miracle to him, but he hadn't given up on trying to reach the fragmented shell that had lived with him for three years, and the young minx had become a handful in the last six years. There was very little she couldn't talk him into, and she knew it. Now he allowed her to take care of him and his household as she wanted.

He descended the stairs, following her a few moments later. As he passed by the kitchen, he could hear her excited tones as she collaborated with the cook and Orpheus. Not wanting to disturb them, he set the empty goblet on the table closest to the doorway then left.

Pausing in the hall leading to the library, Night stared at the unrolled piece of parchment still lying on the stand. He'd already read it numerous times, and he really didn't want to contemplate the meaning of its message again. Against his better judgment, he picked it up and took it with him into the library.

Once he settled comfortably in his favorite chair by the fireplace, Night glanced over the scrawl of his elder's writing. The note was short and to the point. Tere wanted him in the capital in two days. What was so important this time?

Tere had neglected to include that. As at every meeting for the past twenty years, no doubt some of the Dominions would demand an increase in their yearly quota of mortal from the human settlements and cites of Terrasan. Thus far Night's vote hadn't been necessary to keep the petition from passing. Every year each Dominion received ten mortals. With careful care, the number should suffice even the most demanding Dominion. Yet some chaffed under the strictures of the law.

Staring at the letter in his hand, Night didn't really see it. His mind was occupied with his own thoughts. The vampire number of raids on Terrasan had slowly begun to increase.

However, the four Dominions of the lands bordering Terrasan were responsible for the swift execution of any vampires who dared to raid. More than once in the last few years Night had had to leave his home to track and hunt raiders. To his disgust, both Orshan and Valn only diligently hunted the raiders that attacked the cities who provided the vampires with mortals.

Most of the settlements along the border refused to supply mortals and had armed themselves with resistance forces to repel any vampire raiders. Sighing quietly, he set down the letter and reached in his desk for a piece of parchment. Laying it down, he composed his thoughts and as he spoke, the words appeared on the paper. "I will be there as you have requested, my elder. Shall I need a full retinue or will bringing Hawk with me suffice? Your devoted son and servant, Night."

As he folded the parchment, he reached for a small wax bar. He pressed it to the edge of the fold and a small pool formed. Pressing his ring against the melted liquid, it began to solidify, and his mark sealed the letter. Passing one hand over it, it disappeared in a puff of smoke from his desk.

* * *

Night sneered at Orshan, and his elder laid a

restraining hand on Night's arm. The growl wanting free in his throat faded with the touch. Turning to face Tere, he carefully modulated his voice. "You wanted me here, Tere. Must I tolerate that swaggering imbecile as well?"

"I taught you better than that, Night." The hand released him as they moved forward to enter the central council hall. All around the massive room, tiered seats curved along its walls. The imperial command, Tisus, sat surrounded by his guards as the other vampires sought their seats.

Schooling his features to a bland neutrality, Night knew Tere was right. Night rarely attended the imperial meetings. His preference was to remain in his own domain, not bothering with the political nuances and intrigue that so many favored. Following Tere, Night glanced idly over the assembled crowd. Several of them didn't look all that happy to be there. It matched his own mood quite nicely.

As he settled beside Tere, everyone fell silent to await the proceedings. Tisus rose then spoke, his voice carrying clearly to all. "The imperial command has been petitioned to readjust the numbers of humans given to us by Terrasan. While I am not in favor of this, I leave the issue to the floor."

When Tisus fell silent, Orshan stood up. "Many of us can no longer maintain our own domains. Loss due to unexpected disease has decimated my stock of humans."

"Then learn to do the work yourself." One of

the vampires near Night quipped, and his comment drew chuckles from several of the others, including Night. Most of them had heard Orshan's excuses for needing a larger amount of mortals more than once.

A flash of anger showed in Orshan's eyes, but he made a visible attempt to quell the emotion. "I am petitioning the council to increase our allotted mortals from ten to thirty for the duration of two years. After that, I ask for a permanent increase to fifteen."

Deeply resentful at having to be there for the nonsense, Night stifled his sigh, listening to Orshan drone on. The vampire had replaced Reto as Dominion over Reto's domain after Night had punished Reto for his raid on one of the human settlements. A small smirk edged at Night's lips. The fool didn't dare try a raid because his domain bordered Night's, and the same punishment would be reenacted. Night kept an eagle eye on any movements near the border at all times. Instead Orshan forced the other Dominions to listen to his calls for an increase in the numbers of humans every year. Only this time, he'd asked for a triple increase.

When Orshan stopped speaking, Tisus nodded and a moment later, a show of hands rose in the air. As Night lifted his, he closed it in a fist, signaling his disagreement with the petition. Glancing around at the other twenty-seven High Dominions, Night noted fourteen closed fists and twelve palms showing. No wonder his elder had wanted him here. It appeared Orshan had gained four supporters since the last meeting.

Titus held his hand upward in a close fist. "The Dominions have decided to deny the petition."

Orshan scowled at the others as those who had supported him moved from their seats and surrounded him. In unison, they turned to face Tisus, and in reaction, the imperial guards drew their swords.

Venom dripped from Orshan's voice as he addressed the imperial command. "The time has passed for such lax treatment of the mortals. We no longer rule them as we should. There was a time when we had unlimited access to them. Now you think to chain us with your ridiculous laws."

Night now understood why his elder had summoned him to the assembly. The remaining Dominions rose as one and moved to stand between Orshan and the imperial command.

Night stood beside Tere, hand resting on the hilt of his sword. "Has your bloodlust so increased that you must try to force the assembly to allow you more mortals to use? Or is it simply your appalling treatment of the ones you are given?"

Sneering at Night, Orshan had no choice but to back down. Silently the Dominions began returning to their own seats once the tension had been defused. For the next hour, business continued without further disruption. Night remained beside Tere, stilling his own impatience to return home.

When a courier entered the room, she headed straight for the imperial command. As she stopped in front of him, Donay stopped speaking and the others began whispering amongst themselves. After bowing to Tisus, she addressed him. "Imperial, we have received word of a human raid on our territory."

"A what?" A ripple of shock spread outward from Tisus to the rest of the room, and all fell silent. Such a thing had never happened in the annals of their history, and disbelief kept them frozen. Night's disinterest in the proceedings had changed instantly as he waited for the rest of the report.

Orshan jumped up from his seat, angrily yelling, "This is what happens when we don't control them!"

With an imperious gesture, Tisus silenced Orshan. "Continue, Arai."

"Human raiders trespassed on the border property of Dominion Night's domain, Imperial. His guards were alerted and have left their barracks to take care of the mortals."

Night's face remained impassive as he digested the news. What was going on? He'd heard of no recent raid into Terrasan that might explain the bizarre behavior. He stood to address the imperial command but before he could say anything, Orshan started shouting again.

"We will deal with this insolence, Imperial! The mortals that aren't killed will be brought here and divided among the Dominions."

Coldness descended over Night. When he spoke, he carefully enunciated every word. "I will deal with the humans. If you step foot on my domain, I will kill you, Orshan. I will kill any others that dare."

"This cannot be allowed to go unpunished! I demand the Imperial command take steps immediately as a warning to Terrasan!"

"Shut up, Orshan." Night growled the order at him.

Anger suffused Orshan's features as he glared at Night. He opened his mouth to say something, but Tisus' roar silenced him. 'Enough!"

Once silence prevailed again, Tisus continued, "Night, attend to the matter immediately. I expect your reports as soon as the situation is under control."

"Imperial." Night bowed to him before he made his way to the outer doors. It was considered bad form to use any powers in the sacred halls.

Chapter 4

When Night stepped from the portal into his main hall, all was quiet. Striding toward one of the side halls, he entered his commander's office. "What is going on, Lotra?"

"Dominion." Lotra stood at attention. "A party of mortals entered the south section. I sent out a detail to handle them, and they are being brought in now."

"Any details?"

"There were no causalities, Dominion. And the mortals are being imprisoned downstairs."

The door to the commander's office burst open, revealing a rather exasperated, incensed jailer. "He's absolutely refusing to listen to reason," Dorin growled. "Mark my words, this one spells trouble, Lotra!" He seemed to only then notice Night. "Forgive me, Dominion," he said apologetically.

Turning to face the jailer, Night said sharply, "I will deal with all of them."

"Yes, Dominion." They both said in unison as Night whirled on his heel and stalked out of the office. In a dark mood, Night made his way to the lower level of the house. As he opened the door to the confinement cells, he heard the low murmur of voices.

Lotra had known to confine the fighters in the main room. Night wasn't one who believed in the necessity of denying prisoners their comforts. The large open room held several tables and chairs. He noticed most of the humans were sitting quietly or attending their wounded that had been laid out on padded mats.

His medical officer looked up from tending one of the mortals and nodded to him before returning to bandaging wounds. It did surprise Night to note that there were two men occupying two of the cells off to the main room.

"Long day," the medical officer said without looking up again. He gestured absently in the direction of the cells across the room. "Both of them are wounded, but neither will let me near. The blond—Brant, I believe they call him—is just full hot air, I think. The other one…" The officer glanced over at one of the occupied cells. "Well, he's got death in his eyes. He put up a nasty fight, wounded two of ours, if you can believe that." Returning to his work, he continued. "Anyway, he's too quiet, makes the guards nervous. Cowards, the lot of them."

In a quiet voice, Night began questioning the other men. "Was your village recently raided? Is that the reason for this flight of insanity?"

One man stood but kept his distance from Night. "My name is Selwyn. No, our village hasn't been raided for eighteen years."

"Death to the vampires! We will no longer be enslaved to you!" Brant screamed from his cell.

"Silence." Though Night's tone didn't rise, Brant found himself unable to talk.

Enraged, Brant banged his fists against the bars of his cell. The other men in the room remained silent, though several eyed Brant with something akin to disdain.

"He is your leader?"

When Selwyn nodded, Night sighed. "I begin to see. Most of you have been inflamed into this nonsense."

Ignoring the others, he gestured for Selwyn to come closer to him. Night deliberately kept his voice low enough to only be heard by Selwyn. "I will not hold your people accountable for the insanity stirred up. But I will keep yonder hot head and attempt to make him see reason. In the future, if there are any raids attempted on your village, or any others you hear off, send a messenger to me. As long as none of you try such a foolhardy attempt again, you are free to go."

"Thank you," Selwyn murmured. "What about…" He glanced at the second cell. "What about Zach? He won't let anyone near him, not even us. He threatened to tear apart every vampire he saw. I admit that I fear for his safety. He's… an angry young man, sir."

Night walked toward the back of the room to see the other prisoner. Selwyn followed him, remaining silent. "It seems I shall have two guests in my home. I will deal with the matter and see what I can do."

The second prisoner stepped into the light, and despite the large cut down the side of his face, he still looked like he'd kill anyone fool enough to step close. Pale green eyes locked onto Night's, and nothing but pure hatred flashed in them.

"You." The word was growled, low and menacing.

Selwyn stepped back several steps, muttering something about blood-mad men.

Silently Night met the glare pinned on him with a neutral expression. He was no stranger to the hatred of men. "What about me?"

When Lotra entered the main room, Selwyn headed back to the other men. Night's mind linked with Lotra, instructing him to have the others escorted to their village.

"Everybody that can walk, follow me." Lotra instructed the men then led them from the room.

Zach watched every one of them, then his gaze shifted to Night. "I will find a way to destroy you," he said with particular vehemence.

"And may I know the full name of the man who wishes to kill me?"

"Zachary Bern."

"Then, Zachary Bern, come kill me." With a slight gesture from Night the door to the cell opened. Night stepped back, waiting for him.

In a blur of motion, Zach lunged for Night. The barrier protecting Night was the only thing between him and the fire and hatred, coalesced into nearly six feet of muscle. Roaring, Zach pummeled the invisible shield with his fists, seeming to lose no steam in the onslaught.

Realizing this was beyond normal, Night studied the young man, trying to puzzle out something he was obviously missing. He said nothing but let Zach do whatever he wanted, folding his arms across his chest.

"I will kill you!" Zach shouted, never stopping his assault. "I will rip you apart with my bare hands!"

When Night let the barrier fall abruptly, he quickly caught the flailing young man about to fall.

Zach laid into him then, one hand closing around Night's throat in a steel grip. Zach slammed Night against the opposite wall and in a split second had a small but razor-sharp knife pressed tightly to Night's throat, just below his chin.

"Give me one fucking reason why I shouldn't do it," Zach snarled.

Night raised his hand to Zach's arm, curling his fingers around it, but made no effort to disarm him. None of the actions had even really hurt Night. "One, your weapon will do relatively little harm to me. And I must ask if you are in the habit of attacking those who aren't fighting back?"

Taking the opportunity since the young man had gotten so close to him, Night lifted his other hand and ran one finger along the ragged cut to his face. Warmth suffused the skin as it began to heal.

Zach jerked away and stumbled back. He touched his face where the cut had been, then glared up at Night. "Why am I being kept as prisoner?"

"Your own people believed you would be harmful to others. I believe I agree with them."

Knife still clutched tightly in his fist, Zach

stalked up to Night, putting their faces only inches apart. "I did not lead this raid," Zach growled. "But make no mistake: I will find a way kill you. You destroyed me, destroyed my life ten years ago. I will see you dead, even if it drags me down as well. That I promise you."

"I know who the leader is, young Zach." Deliberately ignoring him, Night turned away to face the other cell. A slight gesture of his hand opened its door. "Later you may explain how I destroyed your life. For now, shall we see how brave your companion is?"

The second the door was open, Brant bolted out of the cell, fists at the ready. But instead of attacking Night, he turned abruptly and went for Zach. "You fool!" He landed blow after blow to Zach's face and stomach, but Zach gave just as good as he got, flipping Brant over and slamming the man's head down onto the cold stone floor.

After unfastening his cloak, Night pulled it off his shoulder. As he held it out in mid-air it disappeared from his hand. It amused him to no end that Brant hadn't gone after him.

"You fucking coward! You almost killed my brother!" Several hard slams of Brant's head against the stone and he went limp. Zach crawled off of him, hands covered in Brant's blood. He kicked Brant's side, but there was no movement except for a shift of the body. Zach fell back against the wall, entire body shaking as he grit his teeth.

"Perhaps I should have kept him in his cell. Well, no matter, but it appears you need to clean up. Follow me."

Moving for the door, it opened on its own and Night ascended the stairs. After a few seconds, Zach followed him. "I refuse to serve you."

"Did I ask you to?"

From the top of the stairs, Kat looked down at both of them before she started down the steps. "Night?"

Paying the woman no mind, Zach narrowed his gaze at Night. "What else could a vampire possibly want with a mortal?"

Holding his hand out to Kat, he smiled faintly at her before he answered Zach. "For a mortal of your skills? A servant would be a step down, wouldn't you say?"

Bright, inquisitive eyes studied Zach with a great deal of curiosity as she took Night's hand. "We have a new guest?"

Zach scowled. "What exactly do you intend?"

Ignoring Zach, he patted Kat's hand lightly. "For the time being. Sweetheart, this is Zachary Bern. He will be with us for an indefinite amount of time."

After hearing the name, Kat comprehended little else. Her eyes widened, reflecting open shock. Letting go of Night's hand, she took a step toward Zach, whispering, "Zachary?"

Zach's expression went from pure, unadulterated disbelief, to rage, in a matter of seconds.

"You bastard!" He shoved Night against the wall as hard as he could. "You've brainwashed my sister!"

"Zachary!" Kat's voice raised to a scream as she rushed towards them and began pummeling her brother's back with her fists. "Don't you hurt him!"

More concerned it would be the young girl who would be hurt, Night deftly slipped away from Zach. He grabbed Kat, pulling her away from Zach. "Stop it, sweetheart. That's enough."

"What in the hell have you done to her?"

Doubting he would be believed, Night stayed quiet as he tried to calm the struggling girl. Once she realized Night had gotten away from Zach, she ceased fighting. When Night released her, she stood belligerently in front of her brother. "You can't hurt him. I won't let you. He hasn't done anything to me."

It seemed to take considerable effort, but Zach finally tore his fire-fueled glare from Night. His expression softened as he drank in the appearance of his sister. She'd grown so much. "What's happened to you?" he whispered. He reached out and tugged her to him, holding her tight. "Gods, Kat, what happened?"

"I thought you were gone. That they killed you."

Night remained a silent witness to the touching reunion. The two of them together connected the events for him. Focusing on Zach, his mind connected to the mortal. *She doesn't remember the full details of that night. Or much of what happened after.*

Holding her tighter, Zach scowled at Night.

"You stole her. Kept her prisoner all this time."

Saying nothing, Night moved away to head slowly up the stairs. Pulling back slightly, Kat glared at her brother. "He did no such thing."

"Kat, take your brother to the blue room near yours. He should be comfortable there. And Zach, you will be unable to leave my domain for the time being, so save yourself the trouble."

When Night disappeared around a corner, Zach turned his attention to Kat. "How can you possibly defend him? He's a monster, Kat!"

Hands on her hips, she berated him. "You don't know anything, Zachary Bern."

Whirling around, she stalked toward the stairs. "Your room is up here."

"I know that vampires murdered our family, Kat. I know that he's a vampire. He's no better than the rest of them."

Outrage stiffened her spine as she walked quickly down the hall then stopped at one of the closed doors. Her jaw set in a stubborn line. "You haven't been here as long as I have. I know better."

"I see." Opening the door, he walked into the room. "You've not changed, Kat. Still feisty, still determined, and still naïve. I plan on having a long chat with your 'friend,' and very soon."

"Oh, Zach." She'd never been able to stay mad at him for long, and she wasn't any different now. Before he could shut the door, she launched herself at him, hugging tightly to him. "I'm so glad you're all right."

"I'm glad you are, too. Even if you are still as stubborn as a mule."

Chapter 5

Fire blazed around him, shooting up the sides of the building. Then suddenly the world fell away, and Zach watched in abject terror as flames engulfed the roof. The hold on him was tight, and as soon as his feet touched the ground, Zach spun around and scrambled backward, fear rocketing up his spine as he saw the vampire towering over him. Blue-black eyes regarded him without emotion and Zach tripped on his retreat, falling forever it seemed.

A scream broke the unearthly silence and startled Zach awake. He was covered in sweat, shaking, his heart racing like mad. Wiping his hands down his face, he tried to regain his bearings.

Pieces of the night… day?… before came back to him, little by little.

He'd killed Brant Conner, tried desperately to kill a vampire. Night? Zach blinked. Night. And Kat was here… somewhere. Zach flung the covers off, the chill in the room sending shiver after shiver through him, his hair standing on end all over his naked body.

Seeming to step from nowhere, Night appeared standing beside the poster of Zach's bed. The light of the candle flared from the nightstand. "You had a nightmare?"

Zach bolted from the bed, bumping back against the wall. "What the hell! What are you doing in here?"

"I didn't want you scaring your sister, Zach."

Night seemed unperturbed as Zach nearly bounced off the wall.

"Would give you a reason to compromise her virtue."

"A reason to do what?"

Zach rolled his eyes. "To fuck her."

"Mortals certainly do seem to have dirtier minds than vampires do. You might want to get back under the covers before you freeze."

Barely biting back a chuckle, Night walked to the fireplace and crouched down to place logs from the stand on the hearth.

Blinking, Zach suddenly remembered that he was naked. He snatched the sheet off the bed and wrapped it around his waist. "Then if you're not bedding her, why keep her here?"

"She wishes to stay with me." Night replied as flames engulfed the wood with a snap of his fingers. Carefully he added a few more logs to fuel the fire for the rest of the night.

Zach didn't speak right away. His attention was distracted as he studied Night. He'd been taught—had seen—that vampires were barbarians, monsters; yet Night appeared to be relatively civilized. Grudgingly, Zach had to admit that the man's demeanor wasn't exactly what he'd expected.

As if reading his thoughts, Night straightened and faced Zach. "Don't so easily trust us, young Zach. Now tell me how I destroyed your life."

Night settled at the end of the bed since it was

the only place to sit in the room.

Skirting the bed and keeping his distance, Zach stood in front of the fire to warm himself. Not foolish enough to turn his back on a vampire, he stood in profile, keeping Night within his field of vision. "I was ten when vampires raided our village. My mother was slaughtered while I watched from the top of a storehouse. I can only assume my father and brother met the same fate. My sister was taken — by you."

"Your sister was taken by Reto. As were the others." "It took Night a moment to connect Zach and the full events. "So you were the young boy I pulled from the fire."

"Then how did she end up with you? I've had nightmares since then, and all I ever saw at the end was your face, your eyes. I've had to live with those visions emblazoned on my memory. Not exactly the most wonderful thing to think about for ten years."

"I hunted Reto and the others. By the time I had eliminated them all, I came across your sister and brought her here. She doesn't remember much of that time." An appreciative gleam flickered in Night's eyes as they followed the line of Zach's body clearly visible with the light of the fire shining through the sheet. "You were taken to a family that would care for you. I had no idea Kat was your sister."

"Then I suppose I owe you a thank you," Zach said rather grudgingly. He turned slightly to warm his front. "So you are not my sister's lover, then?"

"You owe me no thanks. And no, I am not Kat's

lover. Nor will I allow another near her. She is far too young for that." Sliding both hands behind him, he leaned back slightly, continuing to enjoy the view Zach didn't realize he was showing.

"I agree." Zach sighed and shivered, the sheet dropping a little lower on his waist.

"You are still cold?" With very little effort on his part, he expended a small amount of energy to warm the room several degrees. "Why don't you crawl back under the covers. I'm not going to do anything to you that you don't want."

"Scoot down." He started toward the bed, warily.

"Are you afraid of what I might do to you?"

"I don't trust vampires," Zach muttered. He let the sheet drop just as he lifted the blanket to get under it.

"I have never forced anyone into my bed, Zach. I certainly don't plan to start with you."

"That's comforting."

"It is? You don't seem comforted at all."

Scowling, Zach shifted several times before he finally got comfortable. "Not exactly."

The faintly seductive edge seemed to return to Night's smile as his dark eyes roamed over Zach before returning to his face. "Do I bother you that much, Zachary Bern? Shall I leave you alone?"

Zach shivered slightly. He was sure if it was in reaction to Night or the temperature of the room. "I'm fine."

"Are you still cold?" Night put his hand on Zach's thigh, and warmth flooded through Zach from the touch.

"Gods… how did you do that?"

"It's just a small part of my powers. Of which I have many. I would have thought your village people would have had more sense than to try to raid vampire land."

"Brant was arrogant, inflaming everyone to follow him." Zach inched his leg to the side, out from under Night's hand. "I only went because my foster brother did."

"Was your foster brother one of the injured men?"

"No. Thankfully. I suppose it is foolish to ask if there might be a place one might relieve himself?"

"Then he should be safely back home by now." He gestured toward the other side of the room. "There is a chamber pot in the small cabinet over there."

Zach glanced at the cabinet and grimaced, as if that wasn't exactly what he'd been hoping for.

Seeing his expression, Night understood the problem immediately. "Ah, I misunderstood your need. Should any of the young women or men find you attractive, I have no problem with it. Until then, I would suppose your hand must do."

A dark flush colored Zach's face and neck, and he cleared his throat. "Thank you," he said, his tone flat. "Under the circumstances, I suppose it's my hand."

"Out of politeness, I should offer to leave. But I am not a very polite person. It would be more interesting to stay and watch you." The glitter of Night's eyes became slightly more heated though he made no move to touch Zach. "Don't worry. I will only watch. I promise not to touch."

"You can't be serious…" Zach met Night's gaze. Why did he feel as if he wanted to give into the vampire's suggestion? It was insanity. Yet the unmistakable throb of Zach's cock showed him to be aroused by the thought of Night watching him. He hesitantly slipped a hand beneath the blanket and taking a deep breath, he closed his eyes. "I can't believe I'm doing this," he muttered, his breath stuttering for a moment. The movement of his hand beneath the blanket was obvious in its slow, up-and-down motion.

"I've always enjoyed others pleasuring themselves, Zach. Not so unusual for my nature. There is something very intense about someone allowing you to watch them in their most private moment." Night's voice seemed to caress over Zach's senses like the feel of dark velvet. "And I don't touch unless you wish me to."

The motions sped up, Zach arching slightly. "Don't stop talking," he whispered hoarsely.

The sound seemed to reach for Zach, tantalizing him with unspoken promises as Night whispered to him. "So close you can almost taste it. It builds in you and shows in your face. So beautiful, so tempting. Let me see you come. I want to breathe in the scent of your desire, to taste it in my own unique way."

"Night." His hips jerked suddenly, the scent of his come filling the space between them.

Night drew his own form of deep pleasure from the taut intensity vibrating Zach's body and etched on his features. As he drew in the scented air, a soft growl erupted from his throat, yet he didn't move. "You smell so sweetly delicious, young Zach. I can taste you on my breath. And you called to me in your pleasure. Such a beautiful sound to me."

Zach licked his lips, shuddering through the last of the tremors. "How do you do this?"

"Do what? I have done nothing but speak to you. I do have a more powerful sense of smell that allows me to enjoy what you just did far more intimately than mortals can."

"How do you make me want you?"

"I have done no such thing to you. And I will show you." Laying his hand on Zach's stomach, the contact sent a sudden surge of near unbearable arousal through Zach. Zach arched and within seconds had Night pinned to the bed beneath him. Zach straddled Night's waist, his cock hardening once more.

It was his own desire for Zach that Night fed to him. Just as quickly as it came, the feeling faded from Zach. "That is what happens when I feed my own desire to you. It is nothing like what you felt earlier, is it?"

Shaking his head, Zach started to get up, but the sensation of silk against his hard flesh was too much. Groaning, he gripped Night's wrists, pinning them to the bed. Without saying a word, he started rocking, the thin fabric the only barrier between them as he pushed their cocks together.

A low groan escaped Night with the friction. It took nearly everything he had to stifle the sound. "Zach, look at me. If you wish, I will take care of that, but push me no further. It may not be what you want."

Careful not to hurt him, Night rolled them both until the weight of his body trapped Zach to the bed. The downward shift of his body parted Zach's legs and he settled between them, running his hands slowly over Zach's inner thighs. The sight of Zach's hardened cock drew a hungry growl from him, he had to taste, if only to ease his own inner need. One hand wrapped to the base before the heat of his mouth engulfed Zach.

"Night!" Zach's fingers twisted in Night's hair, clenching into fists. He bucked deep into Night's mouth, wanting more of the delicious heat to envelop him.

A shudder rolled through him as Zach yelled his name, and Night swallowed him. His tongue and lips began an erotic dance over Zach's cock, hungrily taking him in repeatedly. Just the smallest nick of his fangs to the engorged flesh fed a tiny taste of the hot blood to Night.

Zach shouted, hips snapping up, pushing his cock down Night's throat as he shot. He tumbled hard into the pleasure exploding over his senses. His heart pounded and his body trembled with the sensations overtaking him.

With the last jerk of Zach's body, Night released him. Raising up on his arms, he shifted to the side of Zach. "Perhaps your dreams will not be nightmares, young Zach."

Panting, Zach drew his hands down his face. "Gods. I can't believe I just did that with a vampire."

"It is nothing to be ashamed of. Now you can return to your hatred." Saying no more, Night silently disappeared from the bed.

Chapter 6

Night walked silently down the hall, doing his best to keep his thoughts from straying over what just happened. As he moved down the stairs, the quiet of his home settled into him. It just wasn't enough to ease his mind.

Going into his study, he settled in the chair nearest the fireplace and stared up at the portrait of himself hanging above the mantle. He should have been calling himself every kind of fool. Relations with mortals were at best tenuous. To allow them any depth within oneself was stupidity.

His relationship with Kat was on a far different level. Night had always known that someday he would let her go. The thought pained him because he would miss her presence, but that was the way things should be. But with Zach, the implications would be far different. He'd tasted the young man and only wanted more. That more would eventually build, and Night preferred to head it off before it even took hold of him.

Sighing quietly, he stared into the dancing flames of the fire. Visions of the lush, sweet body lost in passion played in Night's mind. Clearly, Night had been lonely for far too long if a chance encounter made up so much of his thoughts. With a frown, he reached for the nearby decanter and poured himself a glass of red river wine.

For most of his existence, he'd survived on the red waters that flowed through their lands.

Occasionally, he would feed from other vampires, but rarely on humans. To his mind, it was a very bad habit to get into. Quite a few of his brethren disagreed with Night's ideas and found themselves too dependent on the rich, hot mortal blood.

Night's hand slipped beneath his robe. Unable to still the images playing so vividly in his mind, Night began stroking slowly over himself. A shudder coursed through him at just the thought of burying himself in Zach's ass.

The low sound built in his throat and escaped as a soft moan as his fingers tightened around his cock. He could still taste the sweetness of Zach's blood and release in his mouth. Night had known if he had touched Zach in that way, the young man would only hate him all the more.

Something Night hadn't intended to happen, but he couldn't resist the impulse to watch Zach once he'd realized what Zach had wanted. The slow rub of his hand quickened as Night imagined the feel of Zach's ass surrounding him, and he cried out in the silence of the room as he came.

After the tension released from him, he wiped his hand on the front of his robe. A subtle discontent rose in him, and he ignored it. His own hand wasn't what he wanted, but there was precious little he would do about it. Unlike some of the others, he didn't view mortals as toys for his pleasure. His elder hadn't trained him to be that way.

According to their oldest teachings, any kind of

dependence on the mortal creatures had been considered a bad thing. Yet, Night had noticed a growing tendency in his society to ignore that. The problems would only get worse if others like Orshan were allowed to have their way.

Soon it would be time to make his presence more well felt in the capital. A fact Night abhorred but acknowledged as a necessary evil. After he finished his brandy, he stood from the chair. He's spent enough time wallowing in self reflection.

Making his way back to his room, he quickly cleaned up and changed his robe. When he finished, he returned downstairs and headed to Orpheus' workroom. Given his oldest friend's predictable habits, Night knew exactly where Orpheus would be.

Entering the room, he shut the door quietly behind him then joined Orpheus at his table. Scooting one of the stools closer, Night sat down near him but said nothing. Orpheus hated to be interrupted in the midst of one of his potions. So Night waited patiently while he worked.

Several minutes later, Orpheus finally looked up from the bowl of ingredients he'd been working with. "You look troubled, Dominion."

"Before I left The Peak, Orshan wanted to deal with the mortal problem himself. Only a direct order from the Imperial silenced him. Orshan wanted to divide the captured mortals among the Dominions."

"That one is such a fool."

"A fool he may be, but I expect to see more

problems from him. It was a very close vote that defeated the petition to increase the annual allotment of mortals."

"Have they lost so much sense? They are becoming too used to their mortal pets. If they are so fond of them, why not send them to Terrasan and let them live there?"

"It would be nice, but the resulting bloodshed would be unacceptable. No doubt the Terrasans would put them in their place, but not without a lot of mortal lives lost." Most of their kind were wise enough to understand an all-out war with Terrasan would be far too devastating to both sides.

"A more practical measure would be increasing your visits to The Peak, Dominion."

"Something I've already realized unfortunately. I've decided to let Kat return home with her brother. Afterwards, I will be visiting my Elder again." The decision had already been made, and Night was committed to it.

"I assume you plan on leaving me here?"

"You do as well as I at keeping things in order, Orpheus."

"And when are you releasing Zach and Kat?"

"As soon as he convinces me he won't try another foolish act like raiding vampire land."

"From what I've seen of the boy that might be awhile. And you don't look all that happy about it."

Unfortunately, Orpheus could read him all too well. "I knew there would come a time when Kat would leave. But I've never been in any hurry for that time to come."

"Ah, and that's all there is to it then?"

"Of course." Night relaxed slightly when Orpheus didn't continue to question him, but he knew Orpheus had probably seen a bit more than Night wanted him to.

"A visit to the Peak will probably do you some good, Night. At least in clearing your mind. I'll make the necessary preparations, just let me know when you're ready to go."

Nodding silently to him, Night got up from the stool and left the room. The urge to check on Zach nagged at him as he walked down the hall back toward the stairs. He wasn't sure why he tormented himself this way. The young man clearly hated him, and while Night was used to dealing with that emotion directed at him, he found he wished Zach didn't hate him.

As he moved closer to Zach's closed door, he paused. Enhancing his already sensitive senses, he could hear the steady beat of Zach's heart. The sound enticed him and for a moment his own beat in rhythm to it.

Feeling the stir of his own body, Night quietly opened the door and looked in on Zach. He could just see Zach's tousled curls sticking off from beneath the covers. Even knowing he needed to keep his distance, Night went into the room and closed the door behind him.

The sweet scent of Zach's body and blood

surrounded Night with every deliberate breath he took. A hunger rose in Night, wanting the boy for himself, to taste the crimson life more deeply and lose himself in the heat of Zach's body.

Foolish, he told himself as he approached the bed. The tantalizing form was outlined by the blanket over Zach. When a soft whimper rose from beneath the covers, Night sat at the edge of the bed, his hand resting near Zach's hip. Instantly the sound quieted as if Zach sensed his presence.

Could it possibly be? The sound of Zach's sleepy voice whispering Night's name stunned him. Instantly he answered in a comforting tone. "Shh, Zach. You're safe."

Truly bewildered by Zach's ability to feel his presence, Night pushed gently into Zach's mind, lulling him back to sleep. A quiet murmur of contentment reached Night's ears. It should have been impossible for Zach to sense him. But then again Night's heart shouldn't be beating in rhythm with Zach's either.

Night couldn't figure out how it might be possible. Pulling the covers back from Zach's face, Night stared unblinkingly at him. So young and beautiful, yet Night knew he was filled with hate. His hand caressed the softness of Zach's cheek at the same time he tried to ignore the odd draw the mortal seemed to have on him.

His mind tried to convince him that he had misunderstood, but deeper inside something wanted

Night to acknowledge what had just happened. Shaking his head at himself, he couldn't seem to stop touching the young man. It would be best if he sent Zach away as soon as he could. An odd feeling nagged at the edges of his mind, and Night had to shove down the dismay the idea caused.

Zach's dark lashes curved against his cheek in sleep, and Night found the vulnerable, innocence of his face extremely hard to resist. He wanted to show the young man every pleasure in his power to give. To awaken him to the passion shared between two men.

But it would leave its mark on both of them. Something Night couldn't afford. Carefully, he stood from the bed and left the room. It did him no good to linger in Zach's chamber. If anything, it only left him with a longing he had no way of satisfying.

Before he closed the door, he caught a faint sound coming from Zach. Its tone seemed somehow pained, and Night had to force himself to close the door. He knew in that instant the boy had been trying to call him back. Following on the heels of the realization, Night acknowledged that it wasn't likely Zach even understood what he was doing.

As he walked down the hall to his own room, he could feel an indefinable pull still coming from Zach. Night wouldn't allow himself the luxury of accepting just how much he wanted to answer it.

The door opposite his opened and Kat came out into the hallway. "Night, I can't go back to sleep."

Seeing her pale, wan face, Night held out his

arms to her and she quickly snuggled against him. She still occasionally had nightmares and would always come to him for comfort. He opened his bedroom door and drew her into the room with him. "You can stay with me for the rest of the night, little love."

Pulling back the covers on his bed, he slid beneath them, and she joined him. His arm slipped around her as she curled to his side. A small expenditure of his power enveloped her in its warmth and a moment later her steady breathing told him she had fallen back asleep.

He listened to the soft cadence of her breath and the steady beat of her heart. Somehow, he had the feeling he would be lost for a time without his little girl. He refused to acknowledge the other feeling that whispered to him about her brother.

Chapter 7

Night watched from his perch on the parapet as Zach sparred out in the lower yard, going through sword moves. The flow of movement translated to graceful lines of motion with the contracting flex of muscle beneath flesh. An impassive expression settled on Night's features, not allowing himself to show what was truly beneath.

Thrust. Step. Block. Each one was done with precision, Zach's expression focused and serious. Night knew Zach had been avoiding him for three days, never quite making eye contact. But then Night had done the same, except for the moments he watched Zach unnoticed as he did now.

Most times no other understood Night's fascination with humans. But he saw a beauty to the life surrounding them. And in the young man below him it glowed with a brilliant fire. Straightening, Night slowly withdrew back into the house. Zach wasn't his to begin with. At best he could merely teach the young human the wisdom of never straying into vampire territory again.

"I know that look." Kat stood at the bottom of the stairwell, waiting for him.

"You are not supposed to know me that well, sweetheart. Orpheus told me you wanted permission to help him tend to three of Orshan's servants. You may do so."

"Thank you." She walked up to him as he

stepped off the bottom step. "What's been on your mind? You seem distracted lately."

"Nothing is on my mind. Other than what a beautiful young lady you are becoming." His fingers rested beneath her chin and his thumb slid slowly along the curve of her face. "Perhaps soon someone will steal your heart from me. And you will have no more time for this old vampire."

"Night," she admonished gently. "You can't lie to me. Why do you still try?"

"Sometimes it does work. Though I see you are proving stubborn today."

"No more stubborn than my thick-headed brother. He's been aloof and quiet these past few days. Every time I say your name, he growls and walks away. And you grow silent when I mention him. Have you two been fighting again?"

"Sweetheart, your brother dislikes me. He hates all vampires, and you must understand he has good reason." Slipping his arm around her, Night drew her with him toward the central room. "And it does no good to get upset at him for how he feels."

"But he doesn't know you, Night," Kat protested. "He's always been this way, never listening when I try to tell him anything. If he'd just give you the chance, I know he'd change his mind."

"Change my mind about what?" Zach asked as he walked in.

"Some things cannot be changed." Night lifted his hand, pinching her lightly on the cheek. "Now I need to speak with your brother, sweetheart. Go ahead and help Orpheus with the supplies he needs."

"Don't kill each other." With that, she left the room, glaring at Zach as she passed him.

When she was gone, Zach closed the door behind her.

Night opened a crystal decanter and poured himself a glass of the glowing ruby liquid. The remote lines returned to Night's face, and he gestured to one of the chairs. "Please sit down, Zach. I believe we need to talk."

Tossing the sheathed sword onto the floor, Zach dropped into the nearest chair. "I'm listening."

Carefully schooling his thoughts, Night moved to another chair and sat, "When I am ready to let you leave here, I want you to take your sister with you."

"Why? She has made it very clear that she wants to stay here with you."

"Because soon her thoughts will turn to love and marriage. I would prefer to see her with her own kind as she was meant to be."

"As would I." Zach's expression was guarded, unreadable. "And when do you expect to let us return home?"

"You are her family, Zach. All she truly has left. I would trust you to protect her and help her as she grows up. You leave as soon as I am convinced you will not be foolhardy enough to try the same stunt that brought you here."

Zach shot out of the chair, anger pouring off of

him in waves. "This was not my raid!"

Taking a sip from his goblet, Night savored the sweet flavor before he set the glass down. "I am aware of that, but you were dragged into it."

Stalking toward Night, Zach slammed his hands down on either arm of the chair and glared down at Night. "To protect Kurt. I've not given up on my desire to see every damned vampire dead, no matter how much I fucking want you."

Without giving Night a chance to respond, Zach crushed his mouth to Night's, tongue pushing into the vampire's mouth.

The surge of desire that washed through Night was damn near uncontrollable as he felt the bruising pressure of the lips on his. Opening to Zach, he reached up, fingers caressing the side of Zach's throat as his tongue stroked beneath Zach's.

When Zach pulled back, his eyes were wide, a bit wild. He dropped to his knees, fingers working feverishly to open Night's pants. "Need this," he said breathlessly. Unschooled in giving a man pleasure, his enthusiasm more than made up for it as Zach licked the slick drops from the tip of Night's cock.

Night could do nothing but slip further down in the chair, parting his legs to give Zach access to him. The twitch of his cock pulled a shiver from Night in reaction to the feel of Zach's tongue. A vehement bitterness crept into Night's voice as his fingers coiled Zach's hair tightly around them. "I don't care how fucking many of us you want to kill. As long as you do it on your own land, and never return to this one. Do you understand me, Zach?"

"Bastard."

Unable to say anything more, only the vocalization of a growl came from Night's throat with the sweet feel of Zach's mouth surrounding him. A demanding thrust of his hips forced Zach to keep pace with him.

Zach's hands gripped Night's hips, effectively pinning him still in the chair. Then Zach drew back up, tongue sliding along the shaft. He gave the head a hard, sucking kiss, then went back down, the suction strong.

"Zach." Night repeated the name over and over again, and it blended with the rising sound of his moans. A trembling started in him and quickly spread as Zach's mouth set his body on fire. Unable to still his own movement, the push of his hips buried him in Zach's mouth as Night came, yelling his name. "Zach!"

Muffled groans drifted up, Zach swallowing every drop Night gave him. Pulling off the softening prick, he rocked back onto his heels, pressing his palm against his pants. "Night…" He shuddered and his head fell back, hips jerking as he shot, soaking the front of his pants.

Night closed his eyes briefly trying to regain his senses. When he opened them, he saw Zach's face lost in the throes of his own need. The image burned in his memory, never to be forgotten. Edging out of his chair, he dropped to his knees, drawing Zach against him as he buried his face in the curve of his throat.

"Do it!"

Knowing what Zach demanded, Night hesitated. He pressed a soft kiss to the rapid pulse beneath his lips. To taste the sweetness flowing beneath Zach's skin would do far more to him than he could explain. And it would do more to Zach than Night wanted to. He whispered, "No."

Gasping for breath, Zach scrambled backward, landing on his ass. He glared up at Night, chest still heaving rapidly. "I stand by my conviction: you're nothing but an arrogant bastard."

The façade of blankness returned to Night's features. Standing, he straightened his clothing as he looked down at Zach. "Just remember that."

Giving the young mortal no chance to say anything more, Night left the room, shutting the door quietly behind him. It didn't matter he angered Zach. Zach had no clue what he'd asked for, and Night understood that. Heading straight for the stairs, Night needed the escape and solitude of his favorite spot.

Once settled on the parapet, Night watched the sun begin to dip below the horizon. He was as used to dealing with the hatred humans held for his kind as he was dealing with the disregard some vampires had for humans. Lately, there seemed to be an increase in more obnoxious behavior of the vampires. There were still too many of the older Dominions that remembered the far more ancient ways before the law, and they wanted to return to them. They were becoming more vocal once again.

Unable to keep his thoughts on the business he needed to, Night found his mind straying to the image of Zach on his knees in front of him. The young man had absolutely no clue of what he played with. There had been a reason Night had always steered clear of relationships with humans, other than the purely familial relationship he had with Kat. She was like his daughter, and it pained him greatly to let her go though he'd shown no signs of it.

He rarely even fed on them anymore unless he'd been in battle. Humans simply became too attached too quickly, many times whether they wanted to or not. They were too fragile. He could, if he chose, feed his blood to Zach. But that would imprison the young man in Night's world. He would never be able return to his own world, not with things as they were. Too many reasons to shun anything having to do with Zach.

Night stretched out across the stone, paying no mind to the dizzying distance from his position to the ground. Clasping his hands behind his head, he stared up at the darkening sky.

"Night." Orpheus disrupted his quiet reflections as he stepped out of the doorway.

"What is it, Orpheus?"

"The others are being transported to their village by eight of the guards. I gave your messenger to Sarain. She will make sure it is given to the human Selwyn." After approaching him, Orpheus sat down on the ledge near him.

"Thank you. If there is an attempt at retaliation on the village, I want to know about it before the bastards get to the village."

"You think there will be?"

"Orshan wasn't happy that I refused to allow him to step foot in my domain. I doubt he will outright take his revenge. But there is the chance he will get others to do it for him." A possibility that Night had taken into consideration when he'd released the humans. "The body of their leader will satisfy the Imperial command."

"Then what else is troubling you, Night?"

"Kat will soon be returning to her people. Once I am satisfied her brother will hold to a promise of never participating in another raid on vampire territory."

"Ah. I know you have grown attached to the young woman. It is not so easy to let them go." Orpheus didn't appear entirely convinced that that was the real problem. Resting his fingers lightly to Night's forehead, he brushed back a stray wisp of the dark hair.

"No, it's not so easy. She has been with me for nearly ten years, Orpheus. I can't bear the thought of letting her go, but it's what I must do. Her brother will keep her safe."

Chapter 8

Kat sat at the piano, the sound of the music she played drifted in the air. Night relaxed in his chair not too far away from her. He loved it when she played for him. It took his mind off everything else around him.

Zach sat on the floor near the fireplace. He refused to look in Night's direction and kept his attention firmly on his sister. With a slight wave of Night's hand, the lights lowered in the room until only the flames of the fire lit the darkness. Kat could still see enough to continue, and like him, she preferred only the glow and warmth of the fireplace.

The music flowed through Night as he closed his eyes. A bit of smile hovered over his lips. After several long seconds, he felt Zach's gaze on him. Night kept his eyes closed, knowing if he opened them, Zach would look away.

Both he and Kat had spent many of their evenings in this way, but this was Zach's first time to join them. Up until now, Zach had chosen to remain in his room. As tempted as Night was to read the young man's thoughts, he controlled the urge. While Zach still hated him with a burning intensity, Night knew the emotion was confused with Zach's lust for him. They both avoided each other whenever they could, and though Night could have taken advantage of Zach's confusion, he would never do that. The incident in his study hadn't been enough for Night. Nor had it been enough for Zach. Night felt the invisible pull of

Zach's emotions but showed no outward signs of disturbance.

Kat seemed blissfully unaware of the tension between Night and Zach. It was only because she was lost in her music. As aware as Night was of Zach, he felt the smallest shifts of Zach's body as he moved closer to Night's chair. He wanted to reach out to touch him, to encourage Zach, but kept his hand firmly on the arm of the chair.

"Kat, can you play the song mother used to sing to us?"

"I think I remember it. Zach." She hummed softly to herself before her fingers began moving over the keys of the piano.

"Yes, that's the one." The smile on his lips relaxed Zach features, and for the first time Night saw the innocent happiness he'd only seen in Zach while the young man was asleep.

When Kat began to sing the words, Zach joined her, and their voices blended together perfectly. Night listened to them, spellbound. As the two looked at each other, their smiles widened. They were family, solid in their love for one another, and Night could feel the inexplicable magic of their emotions. It brought out a longing in him that he couldn't understand.

Night allowed himself to sink into the pervading mood that enveloped them and closed his eyes. It could always be this way if he wanted it to be. The insidious thought took hold, and for a brief second Night allowed himself to wish it could be.

Kat and Zach continued singing as she played. Night felt Zach's stare on him again. He opened his eyes and saw the longing Zach couldn't hide. More than simple lust reflected in Zach's eyes, and it startled Night. The hatred had momentarily subsided in the young man.

His mind touched gently to Zach's, and instantly a strong pull answered him. Night knew Zach was unaware of what he projected. Zach's own need for Night sought to command everything within Night. The force was so strong on Night, he had to use considerable will to keep himself in his chair.

He could feel Kat's awareness of the current between him and Zach. Still, she continued playing as the mood wove around them.

Their minds remained connected, and the emotional surge from Zach rolled through Night. The deep pain within Zach needed shelter and comfort from Night. As Night slowly stood, unable to deny Zach, Kat stopped playing then slid off the seat and quietly left the room.

Zach stared unblinkingly at him as he approached. There was too much turmoil within him for Night to refuse to give what he could. The instant Night stilled in front of him, Zach came off the seat and went into Night's arms. A pained sob rose in Zach, and Night's arms encircled him, keeping the young man's shaking body against him. Zach struggled with so much. His mind was a chaos of half formed thoughts and emotions. Beneath it all, the raw, open wound of the past.

"Let it out, Zach. You've never had the chance to do that." Night whispered, letting Zach cling to him. In his arms, he knew he held the young child of ten that Zach had once been. His power engulfed Zach, speaking as he once did to Kat, to heal the wounds.

Someone should have helped Zach long ago, but clearly no one had. The young man cried for everything that had been lost that night. His father, mother, brother, sister, and his soul. Night held him through it all. Nothing that had happened had been Zach's fault, yet he'd carried the guilt bottled inside him for half of his life.

Some time later, Zach slumped exhausted against him. Night picked him up and carried him upstairs to Zach's bedroom. Zach desperately held to him, and Night knew Zach couldn't let go of him. He ended up sitting on the bed, holding Zach in his lap as he turned to sit against the headboard. He made sure Zach's mind remained surrounded by a warm cocoon of tranquility and safety.

Many nights he'd held Kat in a similar manner, and now he did the same for her brother. His influence had eased the heavy burden inside Zach, and his mind continually spoke to Zach's thoughts, reassuring and soothing.

Zach fell asleep in Night's arms as he listened to the steady thud of Zach's heart. His own beat in unison, and Night made no effort to still it. Brushing a soft kiss to Zach's hair, Night breathed deeply of the sweet fragrance. An ache had already settled somewhere inside him, knowing Zach would leave.

* * *

Night knew in an instant there were vampires heading towards Zach's village. The messenger he'd sent to Selwyn had been activated, and he could feel its call. He left Zach still asleep and strode toward the stairs as he mentally alerted his guards. Night moved quickly through the house then outside toward the barracks.

When he entered the building, his main squadron were already fastening on their weapons. Lotra, his commander, hurried toward Night as he fixed his cloak in place. "Dominion, what are our orders?"

"Vampires are in Terrasan, near the Rorna settlement. Everybody prepare." As Lostra handed him his weapons, Night grabbed the belt and buckled it around his waist. The others took positions to both sides of Night, waiting silently. After sliding his cloak on, Night waved his hand in the air. Immediately the room phased from view with the wave of energy emanating from Night. A rush of movement flowed through Night as they were transported toward the village.

Night's senses expanded out, tracking the vampires in their locations. There were more of them than Night had thought there would be. He motioned his men into more advantageous positions then waited until their weapons were readied before he released the shielding around them.

They managed to catch the raiding party completely off guard. One thrust of the metal stake in Night's hand sent the vampire nearest him, collapsing to the ground. Any staked would be dealt with later. They had attacked the vampires on the outer fringes of the group and had the element of surprise on their side. Lostra moved forward and his target turned to look back. Before Lostra could silence him, he shouted a warning.

The entire group, who had been marching through the woods, turned to face the oncoming threat. Night spotted the alarmed faces of two villagers right before he drew his sword and advanced on the oncoming raiders. The battle was on.

The clash of swords rang loudly through the trees as his squadron engaged their enemy. The leader was surrounded by a group of me, and Night began hacking his way through to him. It appeared the coward refused to come out and fight his own battle. Relentlessly, Night parried the blows of the three who charged him. His own sword hit home and skewered one of them in the chest. Before he could pull out his blade, a glancing blow caught his side.

Ignoring the pain, Night freed his sword and ruthlessly sliced off his attacker's hand before the vampire could fully bring it back up. Another quick stab to the stomach and an upward yank sent the vampire to the ground. As he moved to deal with the last one, Night senses picked up another stealthily edging in behind him.

Before he could get in a hit, Night whirled. A sudden thrust of his sword to the gut brought the vampire up short. Knowing his other opponent would strike, Night freed the sword and spun fast enough to stop the downward arc of the weapon coming toward his head. Before the vampire could react, the tip of Night's sword pieced his throat, and Night's other hand shoved the stake into his chest.

Night saw Orpheus surrounded by four men. Both he and Lostra responded at the same time. As his commander took on one of the vampires, Night engaged the other two. Neither were anywhere near his skill, and Night easily dispatched them. When he turned, one of the downed vampires stabbed at Night with his dagger. The blade buried in his thigh and drew a growl of rage from Night.

He brought his sword down on the head of the vampire in retaliation. A hard yank of his hand freed the steel from the mass of flesh and bone. Another vampire jumped down from one of the tree branches above and landed on Night's back, forcing Night to the ground. One hand clawed at Night's face as the other stabbed at his back in a fury.

Lostra grabbed the vampire and threw him against the trunk of the tree then ran him through with his sword, leaving him pinned to the wood.

With a growl, Night stood then issued his orders. "Feast on any you will. Make sure the bodies are burned after. Where's the leader?"

"He already ran, Dominion." One of the younger guards answered him.

Night shed form and took to the air. His senses tried to home in on any vampiric aura in the heavily wooded grounds beneath him. When he spotted the fleeing figure, racing back toward the border, he gave chase.

In very little time, he caught up with the vampire then swooped down through the trees. Once clear of the branches and close enough to his target, he took form again. His talons sank into flesh as he grabbed the man by the throat. Rising back up, an iron grip held his victim as a blinding rush of his power forced the vampire to shed form with Night.

Returning to where his men were waiting, Night dropped to the ground and regained form again. Releasing the leader from the paralyzing grip, Night let him fall to the ground and addressed two of his guards. "Take him back to my domain. I want him questioned."

They hastily bound the captive before Night's power could wear off then picked him up.

Standing in the midst of the carnage, Lostra said, "I'll leave Aztar in charge of burning the rest, Night."

"I want you interrogating the leader as soon as we return home, Lostra."

"Yes, Dominion."

"Were any in the village alerted?" Night asked as the forward scout returned.

"No, Dominion. We stopped the two villagers then sent them home once everything was secured. All is quiet in the village."

Satisfied with the answer, Night left the dead and dying for the others to take care of.

Chapter 9

Night followed his guards, emerging from the portal to the open yard of the barracks. Orpheus hurried behind them to tend to the wounded. No one spoke but they nodded to Night as they passed by him to return to their rooms. Covered in blood, Night felt like death warmed over.

He trudged wearily toward the house and went inside, hoping Kat wouldn't notice his return quite yet. She tended to fuss over him, especially when he was wounded. He made his way up the stairs and down the hall towards his quarters.

"What the hell happened to you?"

Night stilled, hearing Zach's voice, and his expression smoothed into its normal neutrality. "I had to take care of a problem."

Zach's eyes widened as his gaze traveled over Night's body. "You're hurt." He left his doorway, stepping closer.

"Not much." Night was being taciturn since his cloak covered most of his wounds. He hadn't expended the energy to heal himself for several reasons.

Growling and muttering something about damned arrogant vampires, Zach grabbed Night's arm and all but tugged Night down the hall. "You look like death. What do you need to heal?"

"I am dead. Orpheus will send up some blood when he has the time."

Oddly enough for him, Night didn't put up much resistance to Zach, which revealed just how tired he truly was.

Zach snorted and opened Night's bedroom door. "You're also stubborn. If it's blood you need…" Zach stilled for a moment, holding Night's gaze. "…then I offer it to you."

Before he hit the bed, Night reluctantly unfastened his cloak and took it off, dropping it to the floor. Several raw, ragged wounds crisscrossed his skin. The gash near his side was long and several smaller stab wounds had left cuts in his arm and back. Dried blood was smeared across his skin, but the injuries had stopped bleeding.

"I won't do that, Zach."

"Why not? Are you so hollow that you can't accept when someone offers to help?"

"I'm too tired to argue." Taking Zach's hand, Night slid back on the bed and pulled Zach with him. His free hand slipped up to Zach's hair, brushing it back from his throat. The sweetest scent filled his senses as he drew in a deep breath. "By the gods, you smell as delicious as the most delectable wine."

Zach shivered, his breath faltering. "Night…"

The brush of Night's lips tasted the warmth of his skin, his tongue tracing slowly over the quickly beating pulse beneath. A soft growl, tinged with his own need, surfaced and his hand released Zach's, burying in the silkiness of his hair. The pierce of his fangs opened the flow of blood before Night's mouth closed greedily over the wounds.

"Night!" Zach's hands fisted in Night's hair, but instead of pulling him away, Zach pressed closer, tremors shuddering through him.

He had known doing this would mark Zach, but he couldn't help that now. The rich, hot blood strengthened him as he drank, and he refused to relinquish his hold on Zach. A deep hunger rose, feeling the weight of the body pushing him into the bed. His hand dropped to Zach's ass, holding him against the rocking arch of his body.

Zach pushed against Night, Night's name becoming a steady, breathless chant. As Night drew back his hand, the ball of his thumb rubbed gently against the spot. Though the blood no longer flowed, two perfectly round holes remained. He stared at them for a long moment before he raised his eyes to Zach's. "I want you, young Zach. To feel your warm flesh surrounding me."

With the words, Night rolled them until he stretched across Zach, pressing him into the bed.

"Yes. Gods, yes. Touch me. Everywhere. Need this."

The slow drift of his fingers smoothed down Zach's chest as he lowered his head, pressing a soft kiss to his lips. "A little patience. You will have what you want."

Edging beneath Zach's pants, Night's hand massaged against the firm flesh of his stomach as he ground against Zach's, increasing the tension between them. Zach arched, hands gripping Night's upper arms, fingers digging. "More."

His fingers eased the edge of Zach's pants downward, then started on his own as Zach wiggled the rest of the way out of his. The feel of their bodies together had Night as hard as a rock.

Bare flesh against his own sent shockwaves through Zach. He threaded his fingers in Night's hair, pulling Night down for a kiss, spreading his legs so that Night settled between them. "Night…" he whispered, stroking one of Night's fangs.

Several shivers ran though Night in reaction to Zach, and the glide of his hand continued to caress every inch of flesh he could reach. The scratch of his fang nicked at Zach's tongue and blood flavored their kiss. Every action was unhurried, and the tip of his tongue teased against Zach's.

Zach hummed, sucking Night's tongue into his mouth as his hands kneaded down Night's back, nails scratching. He shifted his hips, groaning when the motion pushed their cocks together. He rocked up, needing more friction, something, anything to ease the tension building inside him.

Night reached into a small cubbyhole in the headboard. Smiling at Zach, he pulled out a jar and opened it. "A little patience, young Zach. Otherwise, your experience will be a very painful one."

"Need this." Zach met Night's gaze and parted his legs more. Though he'd never done this, he knew very well what happened. He had friends who had chosen men over women; he heard enough stories. And up until Night, he'd never wanted anything so much.

Dipping his fingers into the jar, he coated them then set the jar back down. As he hovered over Zach, he slowly slipped inside Zach's ass. He lowered his head and drew one of Zach's nipples into his mouth, tugging at it gently.

A second finger entered Zach and began stretching him as Night suckled at his nipple. The sweet response of Zach's body increased Night's own need for him, and the touch of his mind brushed to Zach's. *"I can feel how much you want me. You call to me with your body and sighs."*

"Night," Zach growled. His cock leaked steadily, slicking their skin. "More."

Pushing deeper, the ball of his finger rubbed back and forth over the small gland to increase the sensation within Zach. Lifting his head, he whispered, "I'll not deny you when you beg so well."

Zach shuddered, eyes going wide. "Fuck. Night… Please!" He'd never begged for anything in his life, but gods, he did now. The sensations bolting up through him were beyond words.

A slow smile curved his lips, listening to Zach beg. Withdrawing his fingers, he rolled to his back and reached for the jar again. This time he covered his cock with the slick gel then drew Zach up to straddle him. "I want to you to control all of this, Zach."

Nodding, Zach rested his hands on Night's

chest. Reaching behind him, he took Night in hand and eased down, breath leaving him when the head breached him. "Oh fuck…"

"Relax and take a very deep breath." Night quietly instructed him, resting his hands on Zach's hips. He made no move to hurry Zach in anyway. "Guide yourself onto me slowly."

Zach did as he was told, breathing slow and deep. He groaned softly when Night finally filled him completely. "Don't move," he gasped, fingers digging into Night's chest.

Night shuddered before he could still completely. The grip of his fingers tightened on Zach's hip, resisting the need rolling through him.

"Yes… gods, yes." Zach moved, experimenting with the sensations. "Oh, sweet gods… Night…"

Letting Zach choose the speed and motion, Night lay beneath him, controlling his own surges for the time being. He could come just from the tightness around his cock, but he held back. "Ride me however you want me."

Zach took him at his word, hips grinding back and forth. The friction inside him was exquisite, Night filling him over and over. Head falling back, he arched, riding Night faster, breaths coming in quick pants. "Night. I need… now…"

The curl of Night's hand closed around Zach's cock, and he pushed upward against Zach. Night needed very little to send him over the edge, but he waited for Zach. Fiercely focusing his senses on the young man, a soft groan punctuated his words as Night told him. "Let yourself go for me. Let me hear and feel you losing yourself."

"Don't stop, don't stop…" Groaning, Zach came, body jerking hard as he shot, ass squeezing the cock buried inside him.

It took very little before Night came with Zach. The spasms jolting through him and leaving his body shaking as he cried out.

Breathless, Zach slumped down onto Night's chest, shuddering as the last of the tremors rolled through him. "Holy…"

Raising his hand, Night licked off the taste of Zach's release, then his arm encircled him, holding him close. He couldn't regret what they'd had done, even knowing Zach probably would. He simply held tightly to the young man as they both came down.

A few minutes later, Zach lifted his head and kissed Night deeply. Come what may in the morning, they were determined to enjoy tonight.

* * *

Stretched on his side, Night watched Zach as he slept. They'd made love twice before Zach had fallen into an exhausted sleep. His body curled against Night's, head tucked on Night's chest. Zach had proven to be far more responsive to him than Night would have ever thought possible.

Night could feel an edge of pain in the reflections of his own thoughts. He had to shove away any notion of wanting to keep the young man with him. If enough time passed, it would only grow worse. His hand gently brushed over the golden curls as he pressed a soft kiss to the silky strands.

Whether he willed it or not, a bond had begun to form between them. Memories of Zach were already buried deep within Night. Something he couldn't stop from happening. But Zach still hated him.

He knew it was near dawn, and even though the sun had no influence on him, it wouldn't do for Kat or any of the servants to find him in Zach's bed. Reluctant to leave his lover, Night sighed heavily. Very soon he had to send the young man away. Zach's behavior and concern over his sister had proven to Night that he wouldn't carelessly endanger her by attempting another raid on vampire land.

In silence, Night moved away from Zach, and instantly Zach reacted with a protesting whimper as his hand reached for Night. He didn't awaken but clearly he didn't want Night to leave. Night's mind enveloped Zach, momentarily strengthening the sense of his presence as he slid out of the bed.

Zach quieted and Night pulled the covers back over him. Night tried to distance himself, yet something inside Zach called to him. He felt Zach's subconscious trying to pull more strongly on him. Night had indeed left his mark on Zach, and he hadn't meant to. Zach just didn't realize it yet, and with any luck he would outgrow its influence on him.

Without a backward glance, Night left the room and headed to his own chambers. No matter how hard he tried, he couldn't will away the power Zach had over him.

Chapter 10

No matter where Zach was, Night could feel him. His mind followed each and every movement of the young man as Night relaxed in his study. He hadn't been at all surprised that Zach had avoided him in the last few days. No doubt their time in Night's bed weighed heavily on Zach, and there was nothing Night could do about that.

When the study door opened, Night didn't even look up. Only Orpheus and Kat were allowed to disturb him in his study. A smile curved his lips as he caught the beat of Kat's heart. She hesitated in the doorway, shifting slightly from foot to foot.

"Come in, little love." Settling back in his chair, he closed the ledger in front of him. Before he could put it away, Kat rounded the desk and plopped into his lap.

"I am not going, Night. I absolutely refuse to leave you." The determined jut of her chin showed her growing obstinacy to the whole idea. "Zach and I can stay here, can't we? Please say you'll let us."

Night knew this would be coming. How could he explain to the young girl he'd raised that she truly didn't belong with him? Brushing her hair back from her eyes, he said, "We've talked about you returning to Terrasan before, Kat. I've never pushed things when you said you wanted to stay here with me. But you have your brother Zach to consider now."

Tears welled in her eyes and spilled down to

her cheeks. Night sighed as he wiped them away with the back of his hand. "Zach doesn't want to stay here. You know that. You belong with your brother. He's the only family you have."

"I have you."

"I will always look after you no matter where you are." Reaching into a drawer, he pulled out a small box and handed it to her.

Momentarily distracted, she opened the box and pulled out the silver locket he'd had made especially for her. A lone sapphire glinted in the light.

"Only your touch can open it, Kat."

When she saw the miniature of him inside, she gently ran her finger over it. A wavering smile curved her lips.

"If anything ever happens and you truly need me, all you have to do is open the locket and call my name. I will come to you." Taking the necklace from her, he opened the clasp and fastened it around her neck.

"I don't want to leave you, Night." Wrapping her arms around his neck, she buried her face against him.

"I know, little love. But you belong with your brother now."

She knew he was right, but it was so hard to let go of him. A sob caught in her throat and his arms tightened around her as he gently rocked her. Letting a soothing sense of his presence engulf her, he held Kat as she cried on his shoulder.

Several moments later, she'd finally calmed enough to lift her head and give him a wan smile. "You know how much I love you, don't you, Night?"

"I've never doubted it, Kat." Smiling, he wiped away the remnants of the tears from her cheeks. "You'll always have me, even if I'm not there to see."

A light knock sounded at the door, and Orpheus stepped in. "Forgive me for disturbing you, Dominion. The yearly allotment has arrived."

"You want me to get them settled in, Night?" Even though she wasn't happy, she wouldn't forget her duty.

"Go ahead and make arrangements for their rooms while I speak with them, Kat." He let her go as she slid out of his lap. She leaned over, planting a kiss to his cheek before she left the room.

"Orpheus, are they are all healthy?" Night stood, following Orpheus out into the hallway.

"There's a young one in the group I am a little concerned about. As yet his mother won't let me near him."

"And the rest?"

"Scared, but otherwise unharmed."

Night nodded as they walked toward the servants' quarters. He disliked having to deal with this. The only reason he never refused the yearly allotment was because he knew the poor mortals would only be sent back to the Peak and divided amongst other Dominions. He really didn't want to take the chance ones like Orshan would get his hands on them.

They entered the central room and Night saw the frightened humans huddling together. They stared at Night with terror as he slowly walked toward them. Restraining his sigh, he stopped in the middle of the room. Instantly, he spotted the young boy Orpheus had been concerned about.

His mother held him in her lap, glaring at Night in suspicious defiance. Night could hear the faintly erratic pulse of the boy's heart, and the unnatural red flush to his face indicated he had a fever.

"You will not be held prisoner here. I have spaces in my household if you wish to remain. Otherwise, an effort will be made to return you to Terrasan. While I can't let you return to your old homes, you can be taken to any one of several places in the North Valley area."

Silence greeted Night's announcement and the others continued to stare at him in disbelief. The woman, holding her son, broke the silence, her tone clearly antagonistic. "You want us to believe you're not forcing us to stay here?"

His thoughts ruffled unobtrusively through hers only on a surface level to gain her name. He crouched in front of her. "I have no reason to force you to stay here, Mariah."

Studying her son, he noticed the boy couldn't even focus on him. "Your son is ill and needs care. Will you let Orpheus examine him?"

"I can help your son, if you'll let me, Ma'am."

For a long moment she continued to stare

suspiciously at them before she finally nodded. Night straightened from his position and moved back to give Orpheus room. As he attended to the boy, Night faced the others. "For the time being, you'll be made comfortable here until you've all decided what you wish to do. Orpheus is my medical officer, and he can take on any problems that might arise."

Orpheus looked up from examining his patient to nod slightly to the rest of them before he returned to his work. One of the men slowly approached Night but stopped just short of getting too close.

"You're telling us you'll let us go back to Terrasan if we want?"

"Arrangements can be made for that, but it will take several days. Until then, you'll be housed here."

Another woman spoke up. "Ain't got nothing to go back to. They took it all."

Night's brow rose as he eyed her. "Who?"

"The mayor and his cronies took everything I owned and shipped me off to here. They wanted it all and they got it. Not a damn thing I could do since my husband died. Now I can be a scullery maid. What difference does it make?"

"I have no need for a scullery maid, Elisa."

"They took my husband from me." Mariah glared at Night like it was his fault. "I want to know where he is."

Night wasn't at all surprised. Little care was taken to keep the families together unless the procedure was strictly overseen by another who would force the issue. "What's his name, Mariah?"

"Durel Williams."

After she answered him, Night walked to the door and yelled for his commander. "Lotra, I want the full list of names of everyone in the allotment now!"

"I'll be right there, Dominion." Lotra called out from his office and a few seconds later he came hurrying out the door with papers in hand.

Taking them, Night returned to the main room as he scanned over the pages. The mortals had been divided under the names of the Dominion they'd been given to. When he noted that Mariah's husband had been sent to a Dominion that he was more than passing acquainted with, Night looked up from the list. "I'll see what I can do, Mariah."

She didn't look like she took much hope from his words. Night wouldn't make any promises to her that something unforeseen would stop him from keeping.

Orpheus got off the floor and walked to Night. "Dominion, Ales is going to need to remain in bed for at least a week until my medicines have a chance to work in him."

"Then see to it, Orpheus. I'm sure his mother will want to stay with him as well. Tell Kat she has another patient."

Keeping hold of the list, Night left the room to return to his study. He settled in his seat and began dictating the note he wanted to send. "Callor, I see from the Terrasan list, you have a mortal by the name of Durel Williams. I am interested in buying him from you. Night."

While he spoke, the written words appeared on the parchment lying on his desk. After sealing it, a wave of his hand made it disappear into thin air and sent it on its way to Callor.

Hopefully, Callor would be receptive to his offer. Night would definitely prefer to have the family all together whether they decided to remain in his household or to return to Terrasan. Though he'd been occupied, his thoughts hadn't strayed too far from Zach. His senses still tracked the young man's movements in his home. If he focused hard enough, he could feel the beat of Zach's heart at rest.

Closing his eyes, he leaned back in his chair, concentrating on the simple sound. It awoke his own heart, and he could feel the steady thud within his chest. Night could no longer argue that it shouldn't be happening. The sound filled Night's senses and left him struggling against the sudden urgent need to see Zach.

When he caught the sudden acceleration of Zach's heart, Night had a feeling what Zach might be doing. The urge inside Night became too much, and he cloaked himself before he willed himself to Zach's room.

The most exquisite sight of Zach, sprawled on the bed, had Night leaning heavily against the wall behind him. His legs were spread wide, hand wrapped to his cock and the fingers of the other were fucking himself. Night had to exert considerable effort to keep himself hidden when all he wanted to do was join Zach and bury himself inside the writhing body on the bed.

Ragged breaths and moans were the only sounds in the room as Zach pleasured himself. His eyes remained tightly closed and the arch of his body betrayed an unconscious awareness of Night's close proximity. The vampire's name fell from his lips in a pleading tone, and his hips bucked to the tug of his own hand.

Zach shoved his fingers as hard as he could inside him and began frantically pushing them in and out. Knowing Zach wished it was him made things even harder on Night. He reached out his hand toward Zach, but the only thing he could do was heightened the intensity for the young man.

A small measure of his will ruffled over Zach's mind, and the surge drew a sharp cry from Zach. Zach's body strained from the bed then began shaking. The scent of Zach's release filled the room when he came, calling Night's name repeatedly.

Drawing in deep breaths, Night shuddered, tasting Zach's orgasm on his tongue. Wetness stained the front of Night's pants, and he bit at his lips to silence any sound that might escape him.

Chapter 11

Aware of the scurrying movements of his servants on the other side of the door, Night tried to relax in his chair. Everyone prepared to send Kat and Zach back home. He ignored the intrusive sounds as he tallied the figures in the household ledger. The door opened and Kat slipped inside, shutting it behind her. He kept his features schooled to a calm he didn't feel as he smiled at her.

"I wanted to come say goodbye, Night."

As he stood, she skirted his desk and went into his arms, hugging him tightly.

"Will I be allowed to come and see you?"

"Kat, we talked about that before. You know you can't."

"I don't care what anybody thinks." The jut of her jaw betrayed her determined, argumentative mood.

To head off an escalation, Night firmly told her, "No, you will not, Kat."

It would be seen as bad enough that Kat had lived in his household for many years. Night didn't doubt Zach would protect his sister from any speculation. But if she were to return to Night, even just for visits, it would be seen as far worse. Most Terrasans had little liking for their own kind remaining by choice with the vampires.

"We're almost ready to leave, Night." Tears gathered in her eyes.

"You're going to a new life. The one you should have had to begin with, little love." Smiling, he brushed away the tears streaking her face. He knew she wanted to argue with him, but it would do no good. Instead, she silently clung to him, burying her face against him.

When the door opened again, Zach entered to get his sister. He didn't once look at Night. Night had been expecting that, and he released Kat so Zach could take her to the carriage.

"Come on, Kat. We have to leave now."

She went quietly with him, and a moment later the door shut, leaving Night alone. He returned to his desk and shut the ledger as he stared at the closed door. There was nothing Night could do about the situation, though he wanted to demand they both remain. He left the room, heading for the roof. No matter how he argued with himself, Night still ran up the stairs then out to the parapet.

Kat glanced upward as if expecting to see him there. She gave him a small wave before she climbed into the carriage. Zach must have known Night was there by his sister's action, but he didn't once look up. He disappeared into the carriage, and a servant closed the door behind them. A squadron of his men waited patiently on horseback, guarding the front and rear of the coach.

As the carriage pulled away, Kat stuck out her head, waving madly to him. He lifted his hand in a gesture of farewell. Long after she ducked back inside,

Night watched the coach travel the winding road. He didn't move until he could no longer see it.

He'd felt part of himself ripped away as they'd left. Night returned to the house, struggling against the feeling. He could still catch their scents in the house, but in time that would fade.

His stride became more determined as he headed back to the main hall. When he descended the stairs, Orpheus waited for him at the bottom. "Durel just arrived. I've settled him in with his wife and son."

"Very good, Orpheus. Now prepare for the trip to The Peak. We'll be leaving within the hour. You'll accompany me then return here next week."

Orpheus gave him a surprised look, not expecting to leave so soon. He didn't say a word as he turned away to prepare for their journey.

* * *

Night sat on the comfortable pillow, morosely paying little attention to the surrounding atmosphere. Humans weaved between their masters, serving the other Dominions and their coteries. Several were dressed in tunics barely reaching their asses. Whatever colors they wore were the house colors of the Dominion they served.

He had brought none of his household, except for Orpheus, so his Elder had supplied him with one of his own personal servants. Other than occasionally letting him serve wine, Night had waved away the young man.

"Have you become so jaded nothing amuses

you, my dear friend?"

Night glanced over at Bran as the other vampire made himself comfortable on the pillow next to him. "Hello, Bran."

"He's brooding about a human." Orpheus commented, smiling.

"A mortal?"

Night glared at Orpheus, but the older vampire appeared unfazed. Ignoring him, Night turned slightly toward Bran. "He exaggerates."

"You definitely seem out of sorts. Usually, you are far better hiding your disgust at being in Peak. Speaking of which, I never thought to see you here except for the yearly vote. And something tells me he isn't exaggerating."

"It is nothing I'm concerned about."

Before Bran could say anything, they were interrupted by a jovial comment from one of the men in the group approaching them. "Bran, I have another line ready if you're interested. The finest available in Peak. I've kept the lot back to train them and haven't even placed them on the block yet."

Both of them looked up at him and saw the humans that stilled near him. The bevy of young men and women were a clean looking, dressed in the red and blue tunics of Jul-El's house. They seemed well cared for, but then Jul-El had the reputation of taking care of his mortals.

Bran stood and walked down the line, examining each one in turn. He paused before one particular young woman then give Night a speculative look. In response, Night arched his brow.

Jul-El's companion smiled at Night as she rested her hand on his shoulder. "I didn't expect to see you here, Night. Has the country life finally lost its appeal?"

Her warm smile drew one from Night. "Tern has convinced me of the benefits of a bit more time spent here, Shia."

"Ah." She nodded in understanding. "Yes, some of our people have been getting far too demanding. So I agree with Tern." A moue of distaste pursed her lips. "We no longer sell to certain ones. What good is it to care for and train the mortals, only to have all your good work destroyed? Jul-El and I aren't the only ones either."

"I'm pleased to hear that." It certainly explained why Orshan and the others had been desperate enough to push things at the council. Their sources were rapidly drying up. Night silently sipped his wine as the other three talked among themselves. His eyes narrowed on Orshan's, following his circuitous route around the room. He seemed to be behaving particularly friendly and affable to the Dominions who had voted down his petition.

Night smirked when the man nervously glanced his way several times. The display was probably beneath him, but Night took pleasure in it anyway. He simply wanted to remind the fool that he was always watching.

"Do you want me to refill your glass, Dominion?"

The voice pulled his attention away from Orshan, and Night saw one of the young females who had been in Jul-El's line, kneeling beside him. Disconcerted, he quickly eyed Bran.

Bran shrugged slightly, trying to hide his grin behind his hand. "You do need a server, Night."

His friend had roundly cornered him with no way out. "Very kind of you to be so thoughtful of me, Bran."

Night picked up his glass and held it out to his new server. "What is your name?"

"Artika if it pleases you, Dominion." Keeping her eyes lowered, she took one of the jugs from the table and refilled his glass. Once it was full, she set the jug between her legs.

"You do need something to bring you out of your mood, Night."

Night took a sip from his glass then set it down on the table. Bran stretched out on his side in front of Night, eyeing his friend with a great deal of amusement. The others around them were just as relaxed, talking quietly amongst themselves.

When Night reached over him to get his glass of wine, Bran took the goblet from him with a smile and twisted slightly to set it back on table. "I think you need something a little bit stronger."

"Are you offering? Because if you're not, I'll just stick to the river wine."

"Now what do you think?" His gaze held Night's as his hand pulled the hair back from the side of his throat. "What are your oldest friends for?"

"Only you would say that, Bran." The pale expanse of Bran's throat tempted him greatly. Bran's hand slid over Night's chest, further encouraging, and Night couldn't resist. His friend was willing to allow Night to use him as a diversion from his own problems.

Addressing the young woman, Night said, "Go with Orpheus to my quarters and go to sleep. You are excused for the night, Artika."

She nodded obediently to him then replaced the jug on the table before she stood. Orpheus got up from the table and escorted her out of the room.

"She can serve me later, but you will serve me now." He stood, drawing Bran with him.

"I love it when you talk so sweetly to me, Night." Bran pressed against him as the space around them shifted. In a split second they were in the silence of Bran's quarters.

Bran's hand edged between them, cupping the front of Night's pants, and Night instantly reacted. It had been a while since the two of them had been intimate.

Night began taking Bran's pants off. Both of them were already aroused and a lot more than just feeding would happen. He needed to forget what he desired every time he lay alone in bed. He needed to forget Zach.

Undressing each other quickly, they were both naked by the time Night pressed Bran back into the bed. Their joining was swift and savage as Night pinned Bran down and entered him, using his own blood to ease his passage.

Bran's legs and arms tangled around Night, the strain of his body clinging to the jarring force of Night's. His nails slid down Night's back, slicing into his skin, and Night groaned with the pain edging at his senses. Pain itself was an aphrodisiac between them, and the writhing of Bran's body begged for more. "You know what I want, Night. Give it to me."

With a jolting force, Night repeatedly fucked Bran, seeking oblivion. His hand kept tight hold of Bran's hip, sending pulses of painful sensation surging through Bran. He knew exactly what Bran wanted. As much pain as Night could give him.

The sound of Bran's pleasured cry escalated with the burning sensation flooding him. His body convulsed beneath Night as the exquisite rush tore him apart. Biting savagely at Bran's shoulder, the taste of blood filled Night's mouth. He lifted Bran into the brutal motion until his body froze with his own release.

A human couldn't have withstood the damage Night had inflicted. His talons and fangs had ripped Bran's flesh, and his touch continually fed Bran a torturous level of pain. Bran would heal, and he had an addiction to what others would consider intolerable sensations.

When Bran fell back, limp on the bed, Night hovered over him, licking softly at the wounds he'd made.

"You're one of the few who can take me that high."

"You're the only one who would offer such comfort, old friend." Night had unleashed a great deal of his anger and frustration on Bran. A hard-won peace helped him regain his own balance. Night tipped his head slightly, rubbing against the palm of Bran's hand.

"We both needed, Night." The tips of his fingers brushed over Night's lips, and he whispered, "Stay with me this night. I want to fall asleep torn open by you."

It meant Bran had a craving for more serious torment, it would be little likely Bran would leave the bed in the next night or two. He would need all of his energy for healing.

Chapter 12

"You've been missing for a few nights." With a smile, Tere poured Night a glass of the river wine then handed it to him. "And so has Bran."

"As you are well aware, he is still healing."

"So I had heard. Please do not become too distracted to attend the next Imperial gathering."

"I am sure we will both be there. It wouldn't do to earn the Imperial's displeasure."

Pouring his own glass, Tere casually commented, "Uyla arrived yesterday, and she's waiting for a chance to see you."

"Concerning?" Night asked, knowing his only progeny would have filled Tere in on whatever she wanted.

"She wishes your support in gaining a position with the Imperial command."

Night almost burst out laughing. He knew damn well that bland look covered Tere's glee and pride in Uyla's ambitions for a place near the Imperial council. "And no doubt, you've already offered your own as well."

"She stands an excellent chance given the Imperial's stance on the mortal issue. He prefers to have like-minded individuals near him."

The staid little speech didn't fool Night one bit. "Then we must have a small select gathering in honor of the Imperial to show our support of Uyla."

With admirable restraint, Tere nodded in a

dignified matter. "I will make the arrangements, and it will be held in my apartments."

"And I will order several bottles of the best Telsian wine so that you can celebrate privately."

"You know me so well. Uyla did say she would attend tonight so I'm sure she will be here soon to speak to you personally."

Glancing around the room, Night noted the presence of two more of Tere's progeny. "I see Fresa and Nav-Er here as well. How long have you known about Uyla's wish?"

"She mentioned it to me some time ago."

"And you didn't think to tell me?"

Before Tere could answer Uyla came into the chamber. The moment she saw Night, her expression brightened, and she looked like she was about to run across the room toward him. However, at the last moment she seemed to recall proper public decorum and walked sedately across the room.

Setting his glass aside, Night stood and welcomed her with a hug. "Tere has been filling me in on your grand ambitions, darling. I should take you to task for keeping it from me, but I'm more happy to see you."

"I wanted to surprise you." Drawing back, she grinned impishly at him.

"You did that. Does this mean I can expect more visits from you since you will be living closer?"

Perched on the arm of his chair, her hand playfully ruffled his hair as he sat. "I promise you'll see me after the main sessions are over."

When he picked up his refilled glass, she snagged it from him. He reached up, pinching her cheek lightly.

Tere chuckled as he poured Night another glass. "I am going to speak to the Imperial tomorrow night and arrange for the gathering to promote you for the command position, Uyla. Are there any particular people you want to invite?"

"Darsel and Dominion Crusen. They are the two who worked most closely with me."

"I shall talk to Bran as well as a few others to get their support as well." Night took the glass from his elder and raised it in toast to Uyla. "You've done me proud, my fine lady."

"As you both have to me." Tere lifted his glass in toast to both of them.

"I want to try to help ensure the better treatment of mortals, and to make sure the allotment numbers don't increase. You both have taught me well, and I want to stay true to our ideals."

"There is a certain element that might give you a problem once this becomes known, Uyla. Deal with it as you think best, but if it becomes serious enough, I want you to come to me or Tere." Night had no doubts that Orshan and those like him would attempt to bully her into their way of thinking.

"I will if it becomes necessary."

Silently, Night watched the others around them, conversing quietly. Some of them were openly feeding from the mortals near them. He far preferred either the river wine or drinking from another like himself. A second later, his mind acknowledged the lie. No, he preferred Zach's blood, but he still wouldn't have subjected Zach to such a public feeding display. Just the mere thought of Zach was enough to bring back a feeling of empty pain.

Uyla whispered in his ear, "Something is bothering you, my elder. I can feel it."

"I recently sent Kat back to Terrasan. Her brother was one of the mortals in the raiding party that invaded my land. When I found out she still had family living, I decided she needed to return to her rightful home."

"You sent Kat away? Knowing her as I do, I doubt she liked it all that much."

"No, she didn't. But it is where she belongs."

"I don't think that's all that is troubling you, Night. There's something else."

Night could feel the tentative mental touch from her. He'd never shut her out before and wouldn't start now. Reaching for his hand, she stood and pulled her with him. Bowing to Tere, Uyla said softly, "Please excuse us."

Inclining his head to both of them, Tere waved them off. Uyla didn't say anything as they left the room then walked down the outer corridor to the stairs leading outside. The Peak was a city within itself, populated by vampires and the Terrasans that served them. Walking along the cobbled street, Night drew in a deep breath of the night air. Varied scents from the main bazaar perfumed the air, and Night could detect the delicate fragrances of magical herbs along with the honeyed aroma of red river wine.

When they entered the market, Uyla began browsing among the stalls. "I hope you will tell me what is troubling you, Elder. It never does you any good not to."

"It is not a matter of importance, Uyla." Night murmured in answer. It had been enough of a battle to subdue how he felt about everything. It simply wasn't in his nature to really want to talk about it.

Laying down the gossamer red skirt she had been contemplating, Uyla turned to him. "Who is the mortal you are in love with?"

"Kat's brother."

"Why isn't he with you now? And please don't give me the 'we aren't meant to love mortals' speech. That's the worse piece of nonsense I've ever heard."

"It isn't so simple. It never is. Zach hates our kind more than most Terrasans do. For good reasons of his own."

"Does he even know what you feel, Night?" Her tone softened affectionately over his name.

"No, I doubt it would have done much good. Both Kat and Zach belong in their own world, not this one. It is a dilemma with no answer, Uyla. Wisdom is in accepting that."

She returned to browsing amongst the fabrics then asked as casually as she could. "But what if he does come to return your love, Night. What would you do then?"

Surprised by the question, Night floundered for an answer. It really wasn't something he'd considered at all. "That is never likely to happen."

"But if it did?" Uyla continued to push him. After she asked, she chose a beautifully embroidered black and silver dress and headed toward the market seller to pay for it.

Night caught a glimpse of what it might be like to have Zach back in his arms. A painful ache rose in his heart with the question haunting him. As much as he longed to have Zach with him, he wasn't sure he could fully accept the differences between the two of them. No matter what he felt, mortals and vampires simply weren't meant to coexist in such an intimate level.

His relationship with Kat had been far different. He'd merely stood as a father figure to the young girl. Night had become very attached to her on an emotional level, but he recognized there was no sense of permanency to them. When Uyla returned, they continued shopping in the bazaar, but their conversation became more general.

* * *

Night had waited several moons for the partial session that was about to begin. Orshan had made an open call for the meeting, and Night decided to attend it. Settled in the back of the room, he listened to the flow of conversation around him. Complaints about the lack of humans to serve them seemed to be the main topic.

Orshan hadn't yet shown up, but Night noted quite a few prominent members of the Dominion Counsel. As to whether any were there in support of Orshan or for the same reasons he was, Night really wasn't sure. With that in mind, Night made note of those who were being vocal about the problem and those who weren't saying a thing.

When Orshan came into the room and stepped into the speakers' square, the room fell silent. "My fellow Dominions and citizens, it's long past the time that we stop treating the Terrasans as if they are special creatures. The old laws no longer serve us, and it is time for us to break away from those who support it.

The Imperial has decided to ignore our petitions for an increase in the allotment. I say it's time we make our own laws. The Terrasans are meant to serve us."

Several of the crowd held up their arms, hands open to silently show support. There were quite a few who showed open disgust at the ideas Orshan presented. A call for others to break off from the main body of the government wasn't highly unusual. Nor were harsh criticisms of the Imperial. But Night doubted if Orshan planned on giving up his prestigious Dominion position in order to start a new utopia of his own.

Once Orshan had finished, some began leaving the room as others headed down to the speaking floor to congratulate Orshan. While Orshan might have been a growing nuisance when Tere first brought Night's attention to this, now he'd become decidedly more dangerous in Night's eyes.

Orshan noticed him sitting in the upper rows, and mockingly saluted Night. Standing slowly, he met Orshan's gaze with a chill disdain. Brushing past the others, Orshan came up the steps and stopped in front of Night. "Either you are with us, or you are dead."

"Orshan, it is never wise to threaten those who would truly kill you with no hesitation." Bowing, Night smiled in an amused fashion at Orshan as Bran came up behind Night. Bran's menacing growl increased the sudden tension.

The other vampire abruptly turned to the side and stalked away. Half turning, Night eyed Bran. "I had no idea you were here as well."

"Somebody has to watch your back." With a shrug, Bran took Night's arm, and they left the session hall.

Chapter 13

Things were no longer the same. Zach sighed as he sat at the tavern table, nursing his mug of ale. The talk around him was of the coming season, the harvest and Noctia festival. Life seemed normal for everybody around him, except for Zach.

Kurt lifted his cup, eyeing his Zach over the rim. After taking a healthy swallow, he asked, "Are you going to ask Luci to the festival?"

"Hadn't thought about it, Kurt." In the three months since they'd returned to the village, everything seemed to have changed for Zach. He'd also noticed Kat wasn't having that easy of a time of it either.

Nobody in the village ever mentioned the failed raid or the death of Bran. The participants had returned to their old lives and conveniently obliterated any memories of what had happened. Zach wished it could be so easy for him.

"Maybe I should ask her then. She is a sweet handful." Kurt smiled to himself, clearly distracted by his thoughts. "Or maybe I could ask Kat. Do you think she'd say yes?"

Making an encouraging sound, Zach drank from his mug. He had a great deal more to think about than the harvest festival. Although his sister had tried to fit in when they came home, Zach could tell she wasn't happy. But then neither was he.

Setting down the mug, Zach stood. "I'm going to go check the south field then find my sister."

"Tell Mom and Dad I'll be home later. I'm going to go talk to Raine. He's setting up the next resistance meeting."

Zach nodded to him before he made his way out of the tavern. There wasn't a day that went by that his thoughts didn't dwell on his illicit lover. Any relationship between a vampire and a human simply wasn't acceptable in his world.

Walking slowly down the lane that led from the village to his father's farm, Zach barely paid any attention to what was around him. Just the thought of Night made him ache, an unbearable need that rose unbidden and tortured him with the memories of the feel of Night inside him.

But it was far more than that. Some part of Zach knew it, yet he refused to acknowledge it. When he reached the south field, Zach walked the perimeter, checking on the planted crop of black field berries. Their distinction fragrance already permeated the air, indicating they were close to harvest time.

Once satisfied with the progress of the crop, Zach walked over the rise leading to the back woods that bordered Markus' land. He knew his sister spent more time wandering the woods than she did in any other place. Either he would find her picking wild berries in the silent grove or down by the creek, eating them.

Because of superstitious belief, nobody ventured anywhere near the silent grove. The eerie lack of sound made people too nervous. It had never bothered him, and he wasn't surprised when Kat took to hanging out there as well.

Ancient stones, tall and slender, ringed an enormous, circular area. Vines and bushes nearly obscured the stones from sight, but Zach knew the strange carvings on them by heart. He'd spend many hours studying them. Trees grew in the outer ring outside of the stones, but none grew within the circle. Only flowers and bush after bush of different kinds of berries grew in the clearing. No doubt magic of some kind, and probably long forgotten as well.

Reaching down, Zach paused long enough to pick a handful of bright purple berries before he followed the meandering path down to the creek. Once outside the circle, only the sounds of the animals inhabiting the woods accompanied him. Soft trills sounded in warning from the birds in the branches above him as he passed by. It was completely peaceful out here, and Zach had spent a great deal of time exploring the area when he was younger.

Popping a couple of berries at a time into his mouth, Zach savored the sweet burst of flavor over his tongue as he walked the overgrown path. On a small rise above the creek, Zach spotted his sister, sitting at the edge of the water and eating from the pile of berries tucked in her skirt. Her hair was mussed, looking as if it hadn't seen a comb all day long.

"Kat." He called out as he walked down the incline toward her.

"Figured I'd find you out here." Laughing,

Zach plopped down beside her then took off his shoes. After setting them beside him, he put his feet into the cool water.

"I like it out here, Zach. It's so beautiful and nobody is around."

"Has anybody been giving you any trouble, sis?"

"No, not really. It's just hard to get close to any of them. They don't like the same things I do." She picked up the bag beside her and opened it for him to see inside. "Look what I found. It's really hard to get dark thistle, but I found a whole field of it. I can use this to make an ointment for sores. Orpheus was always running out of that."

At her mention of the vampire, Zach looked away from her to the placid running water of the creek. After she dropped the bag, Kat sat up, laying her hand on his arm. "Zach, you don't talk about them at all. Why?"

There was no way Zach could think of an answer that would satisfy his sister, and he knew it. Instead, he remained silent and fixated on the water.

"I know you love him, Zach. Why won't you talk about it?"

Her words startled him. Even before he spoke, Zach realized he couldn't deny what she'd said. He'd known the truth before he left Night and had refused to accept it. "I love him, but it's not acceptable, Kat."

"To whom?"

"You know what everybody would say. We

aren't meant to be with them."

"Who cares what anybody else thinks? This isn't about them. It's about you and Night, Zachary Bern. Don't you even realize he cared about you?" Scowling at him, Kat moved to her knees and got in his face. "I could see what it did to him when we left, but you didn't even look at him. Why? Because nobody in this place would approve?"

"No, Kat, you don't understand. I didn't want to feel this way. It's against everything I believe in."

"Then change what you believe. Everything you thought about Night and his kind was stupid in the first place. Yes, some vampires are bad. Like Orshan and others like him. But Night didn't deserve the way you treated him. He doesn't treat our kind like slaves, he never has. He really didn't want us to leave. I know he didn't."

Grabbing his upper arms, Kat turned him to face her. "Are you happy here, Zach? Because I'm not. I want to go home where I belong. Please."

The earnest, pleading look on her face affected him deeply. He considered what to say for a long moment before he spoke quietly. "Give me some time to think about it. All right, Kat?"

"As long as you'll think about it."

"We better go back to the house. I'm pretty sure Harriet has dinner ready. They're probably waiting on us." Untangling himself from his sister, Zach took her hand and stood, helping her up. "You know Kurt is thinking about asking you to the festival dance."

Her brow wrinkled in puzzlement as she walked beside him. "Why would he want to ask me?"

"Maybe he likes you." Zach couldn't resist teasing his little sister about it. "He does hang around us quite a bit. More than he used to be around me."

"Most of the time I see him trailing after Luci and her sister. You sure he wasn't kidding you?"

"I'm pretty sure. Kat, Luci is a beautiful girl, but she thinks of little outside of herself. Maybe Kurt is starting to realize that." He shrugged then fell silent as they neared the house and went inside.

* * *

Several days later Zach trailed his sister as she shopped in the market stores, and Kurt tagged along with them as well. They both waited patiently as Kat happily looked over the displays of sugar and chocolate confections. As Zach rested against the counter, he talked to the store owner while Kat made up her mind. "The crop of black field berries should be ready for harvest soon, Elly. Did you want to put in an order?"

"I'll need at least seven cues, Zach. With the harvest festival coming up, I expect we'll run out of the hard candies very quickly. Any chance of you bringing in some pink and purple grove berries?"

Because nobody else would go to the grove to pick them, Zach had made a bit of a side business for himself in picking them and selling them to the local businesses. "The purples are already at peak. I'll bring you some tomorrow. Pinks won't be ready until closer to the harvest."

"That's good." Pleased, she nodded to him then moved back to the counter to get Kat the candy she wanted. Once Kat had selected everything she wanted and it was bagged, they left the store.

"Zach, I was wondering if we could stop by the flower shop. I think Boran might be interested in buying some of the grove flowers. What do you think?"

"I never tried so it won't hurt to ask him. Are you going to help me pick the grove berries? We'll share the gold between us." When she opened the bag, Zach reached in and plucked one of the chocolate burns for himself.

"I'd love to, Zach." As they passed by a group of other young people, Kat nodded politely to them.

"Zach, will you be going to the harvest festival?" Luci asked him flirtatiously before she glanced at Kurt. "And what about you, Kurt?"

Stopping to converse for a moment with them, Zach answered her question. "Not this year, I'll likely be too busy working."

Simpering at him, Anla placed her hand on his arm, fluttering her lashes at him. "Surely your father will let you attend the night of the harvest dance."

Kat stayed back, preferring to be ignored by the women and men since she'd never felt comfortable around them. It didn't help that they seemed to look down on her because she'd been raised in the Dark Territory.

"I know Kurt will be going, Anla. If I have a chance, I will probably bring Kat to the dance." Glancing over his shoulder at his sister, he stepped back and slid his arm around her. "We better get the rest of our shopping done before the stores close."

"We're meeting at the tavern tonight, Zach."

"We'll be there, Royn." With a nod, Kurt continued down toward the flower shop.

"If you want to speak to Boran, go ahead. I need to stop by the bakery to get Erne's order. Kurt, go ahead and see if Ang is going to put in an order this year."

"It shouldn't take me too long, Zach." Kat walked away from him, entering the florist shop as they other headed in opposite directions. Entering the bakery, Zach stood to the side while Erne waited on a customer. Glancing over the wide selection in the glass cases, Zach decided to get his foster mother one of the beautifully decorated cakes. He enjoyed surprising Harriet with little gifts for absolutely no reason.

When the other customer finished, Zach stepped up to the counter, pointing to the cake he wanted. "Wrap that up for me, Erne."

Nodding to him, Erne reached into the case and picked up the cake. As he put it in a special container, he asked, "You ready to start taking orders for the harvest, Zach?"

"That's really why I came in. The black field berries are about ready for harvest and so are the grove berries. How many of which do you need?

"Got my list right here." Grabbing his pad, Erne flipped it open. "I'll need at least 50 cues of the black and 75 of the red. I saw you and Markus put in some of the yellows in the back field. Last year, I sold out of them too fast. I'd like to double my order if you planted enough."

"We can do that, Erne. You want any grove berries?"

"Bring me what you can of those, Zach. I've a special display ready for them this year."

"I'll get as many as I can then." Waving farewell to him, Zach went back outside. Not seeing Kat, he decided to pick up one last order at the food market. Zach went into the store and talked for a short time with Kalya, taking her order for berries. All in all, it was proving to be a very productive day. After he left the store, he saw Kat and Kurt by the bakery shop and joined them.

"You can add 20 cues of black and 10 of the yellow for Ang, Zach." Kurt barely got that out before Kat broke in.

"You're not going to believe this, Zach. He wants as many flowers as I can bring to him." Kat excitedly told him. "Boran said he could make up special bouquets for the men to give their sweethearts for the festival. When I left him, he was already making plans for it."

"Then we'll be very busy in the coming days." Zach smiled to himself, seeing the appreciative gleam in Kurt's eyes as they rested on the animated Kat. It didn't surprise him all that much when Kurt decided to walk beside Kat, and he was left trailing after them.

Chapter 14

"Thank you, Kat. These look delicious." Erne eyed the selection of grove berries she'd brought him. "I'll have to work a bit of overtime so they don't spoil, but it'll be worth it."

"I can prepare them so they don't spoil so quickly, Erne."

"I can't afford Berma treatments. It would raise my prices too outrageously."

'Oh no, Berma is way too expensive. I was thinking about another treatment. It would cost you one extra gold per cue." It hadn't occurred to Kat that the villagers didn't have access to the cheaper methods of preventing food spoilage. Orpheus had taught her several methods because the use of Berma wasn't cost ineffective in keeping humans fed. Both Orpheus and Kat preferred to spend the money on a higher quality food, rather than on preventing spoilage of lower quality food.

"Only one gold?"

"I can treat the berries so they don't spoil, and you won't have the problem Berma can cause. Berma does prevent spoiling, but it can sometimes make the produce too bitter if it's not used after a certain amount of time."

"Go ahead and treat the next batch for me, Kat. Can I store the excess for winter usage? If I can, double the order for me."

"The berries would be safe to use until the next

harvest, Berne. I'll have the next batch to you soon."
She left the store in a thoughtful mood and caught up
with her brother who was leaving the tavern.

"Zach, I just realized that none of the store
owners know how to prevent food spoilage, other than
using Berma."

"That's true. Since this isn't the city, most can't
afford the ten-gold cost of Berma."

"I think I can help with that." She tucked her
hand in his arm, pulling him toward home. "Orpheus
taught me how to use pink Rosia weed. It's not
harmful at all and doesn't leave a bitter taste like
Berma can. There's an entire field of Rosia weed down
near the creek."

"How do you use it?"

"It's really simple. You pick the pods then cut
out the seeds. All you do is ground the seeds and then
heat them to dry. It would only take a few grains of the
powder in water to treat what we've picked. It
wouldn't take more than a pod to treat all the berries
we'll get from the grove."

"Do you think the same could be done for the
field berries?"

Kat had an idea of what Zach was thinking.
"Sure. The field I saw was more than enough to treat
Markus' fields, plus lay in a supply of the Rosia
powder for quite a while. I charged Berne an extra gold
per cue, and he was fine with it. Markus would be able
to do the same. It wouldn't cost him anything except
time and a bit of extra work to treat the berries."

"I think we need to discuss it with Markus." Zach quickened his step and several moments later they entered the kitchen. The aroma of Harriet's soup and fresh baked bread made both of their mouths water.

"Sit down, both of you, before the soup gets cold." Harriet fussed around them, filling their bowls with soap and setting plates of sliced bread beside them.

"Thank you, Harriet. It smells really good." Kat picked up a knife and buttered a piece of bread.

"Markus, Kat was telling me about a way to treat the berries for spoilage. I think it might be a good idea. Go ahead and tell him, Kat."

"You can treat the berries with Rosia weed. There's a field of it down by the creek, so it wouldn't cost you anything for the powder. I offered to treat Berne's next batch of grove berries for him and charged him an extra gold per cue. Tomorrow I'm going to talk to Elly and Kalya."

"I've never heard of using Rosia. How much would be needed to treat the field berries?"

"You'd need three pods for every cleaning vat, Markus. You already cleaned the berries. You'd just have to let them soak for a day in the water instead of just rinsing the berries off. The berries will last until next harvest, and they won't get bitter like they would if you used Berma. You do have to keep the vats covered from the sun since light will break down the effectiveness of the powder."

"That wouldn't be difficult at all. I'd have to buy a few more vats, but increasing the cost to one gold per cue would more than cover that."

"Next year, you could consider doubling your crop and storing the berries. Then take them into the city to sell in the winter. You'd get even more gold there." Zach added his own suggestion.

Markus started laughing, clearly delighted with Kat's plan. "I'd definitely be able to sell the cues for far less than the city stores. This is a very good idea, Kat."

"I can pick and prepare enough of the Rosia powder and show Harriet how to do it. It's not that hard. There will be more than enough to treat your fields with plenty left over. You can also grow Rosia weed as well to keep supply on hand."

"Zach, talk to everybody and see if they want their field berries cues treated. I think we should talk to some of the other farmers as well. To see if they wouldn't be interested in buying the powder to treat their own crops. You think there's enough Rosia weed, Kat?"

"I think so. It's a large field, but I'd need some help picking the pods."

Zach smiled to himself, seeing how excited his sister seemed to be. He hadn't seen her so relaxed and happy since they'd left Night.

"Kurt and Zach can help you. Our harvest will be around two thousand cues this year. Since we need to soak the berries, I'll have to get at least five more vats." Standing, Markus went to his work desk for a pen and paper.

"You'd bring it about two thousand more gold, Markus. Five vats would only cost two hundred and fifty. I'll make the rounds of the other villages and the farmers to see who is interested." Zach sat back after he finished his soup, rather satisfied with the whole discussion. It would increase Markus' profits and allow him to expand as well. Most likely it would have the same effect on the rest of the farmers in the area.

"I'll go ahead and get some of the berries and Rosia picked." Having finished her lunch, Kat stood from the table and headed outside to the harvest shed then began filling the small cart with several baskets. With the berries so close to being fully ripe, she needed to pick as many as possible to fill the orders. Since Zach would be busy helping Markus in the south field, she was on her own today. When she turned to get another basket, she saw Kurt leaning in the doorway, watching her.

"Are you going to need any help, Kat?" he asked with a smile.

"If you can spare the time. I need to fill all of these baskets, plus get some Rosia weed so I can start processing it for the vats." Pausing, she gave him a shrewd look. "Are you sure you want to go to the silent grove."

"It's never really bothered me." Kurt shrugged as he pushed away from the door and picked up several baskets.

Since it wasn't the first time Kurt had

volunteered to help her out, Kat said nothing and just continued loading the cart until they were done. Kurt pushed the cart, walking beside her as they headed down the lane toward the grove. "I told mom I'd have you teach me how make the Rosia treatment. The more we have, the more we'll be able to sell to the rest of the farmers."

"That's fine." Kat continued to walk silently, aware of his gaze on her. When she glanced at him, he opened his mouth to say something then quickly shut it.

"Kurt, is there something you want to say?"

"Not really." He seemed to think second of his answer then said, "Well, yes, but I'm not sure how you'll take it."

Kat turned down the small path leading to the grove. "Why don't you just ask and see if I'll answer."

"Because it's about your time with the vampires, Kat. Neither you nor Zach has said anything about it." He gave her a questioning look.

"I don't mind talking about it, Kurt. I just didn't think anybody would listen to me, because it's not like people around here think." As Kurt pushed the small cart into the grove, Kat considered the best way to explain everything to him.

They both grabbed a basket and began picking the berries from the bushes, then worked side by side in silence for a few moments before Kurt spoke again. "You can talk to me. I promise I'll listen to you."

"It really isn't like people think. Some of the

vampires are bad, like Orshan. His domain borders Night's. But Night always treated me and other mortals with great care. His Elder is the same way. Night never, ever mistreated me or hurt any of the others." A fond smile crossed her lips with her reminiscing. "In fact, Night loved me, just as my own father did. He was the one that found me after I was kidnapped."

"I saw him when we were taken to his keep. It surprised me that he didn't kill us immediately."

Kat gave him a horrified look. "Night would never do something like that, and he always let me help the servants Orshan badly treated. He would never kill someone without just cause, not even mortals."

"An attempted raid on his territory would have been just cause to many." Kurt quipped drily.

"Clearly it wasn't to Night."

"He spoke to us before he returned us to the village, Kat.

"Not all of them are the same, Kurt. I know that his Elder, Tere, and his daughter, Uyla, work with some of the cities in the south. They don't force mortals to go to the Dark Territory. And Night only takes mortals from the yearly allotments so they won't be mistreated elsewhere. A lot of times he sends them back here to new lives."

As they continued to work together, Kat told him more about her own life with Night. It was a relief to be able to freely talk about it. Nobody else would have been willing to listen to her about any of it.

* * *

On the night of the Noctia dance, Kat and Zach sat on the sidelines content to watch the others whirling gaily past them. Markus sat among the other farmers, talking about their plans for expanding their crops for the next harvest. Kat's idea had gone over with a resounding success. In gratitude, Markus had given Kat half of what he'd taken in with a promise to share future profits.

The only thing left was to talk to Markus about returning to Dark Territory. True, they'd both been happy the last few weeks. But they'd been too busy to dwell on anything else but the harvest. Now Zach's thoughts began to turn more often to the subject.

"Zach, have you thought about going back to Dark Territory?"

"Yeah, I have. I haven't thought of much else. I wanted to wait until the harvest was over to talk to Markus." Every night his dreams had been haunted by the memories of Night, and he'd welcomed that. At least they wouldn't return to Night empty-handed. They had both taken in quite a bit of gold this harvest.

"Then I can start getting ready?" A gleam of excitement lit her eyes as she practically bounced beside him.

"Yes, Kat, you can."

Neither of them had much interest in remaining at the festival. Kat left his side long enough to sample food from the tables that had been carefully prepared.

She returned with a small basket laden with goodies. "We have enough for our journey, dearest brother."

"I suppose we should return home to pack and get a good night's rest before we leave."

"Best suggestion I've heard since we left Night." She grabbed his hand and pulled him out of his seat.

"Let me talk to Markus then we'll leave." Laughing, he freed his hand and walked over to his foster father. After a quietly voiced conversation, Zach promised he would explain everything more fully to Markus in the morning. Before he returned to Kat, he noticed Kurt had actually convinced his sister to go to the dancing circle. Surprised, he leaned back against the wall, holding the basket as he waited for her.

His sister was flushed and laughing when she left the dancing area. Rejoining Kat, they left the festival and began to walk home. Kat's hand curled around his as she gave him a side glance. "He's worried about you."

"I know. Markus doesn't know Night as we do. He really doesn't want us to go back there."

"I don't think you can tell him the full truth, Zach. But I believe Harriet will understand. She's asked me a few times about what's bothering you. I didn't tell her, but I have the feeling she knows there is someone you love."

With her words, Zach realized it might be easier to explain things to his foster mother. He knew she would help him with Markus. It was more likely she would accept he was in love with a vampire and would help her husband to understand as well.

When they got back to the house, Kat went to her room to begin packing, and Zach headed to his. They wouldn't take much with them. No more than a few changes of clothes, their gold, and some food. Zach planned on traveling light so they would get to Night's domain as soon as possible. Traveling through Terrasan with the intention of going into Dark Territory would be dangerous.

After choosing the clothes to take with him, Zach stuffed them into his pack and included the dagger Markus had given him. There were a few personal things he absolutely refused to leave behind. One was the dagger and the other was a special metallic disc that had been engraved as a portrait of his family.

He finished the task of packing quickly then undressed and stretched out on his bed. Thin ribbons of moonlight streamed into his room, and he listened to the quiet, comforting sounds of the nocturnal animals outside. A deep sense of excitement welled up inside Zach. Soon he would see Night again.

A shiver ran through his body in response to the thought, and Zach rolled to his back to muffle the sound of his groan. The dark eyes that had always haunted him through his life had become a pleasure instead of a nightmare.

Every part of him longed to see those eyes again, to watch Night's face as he became lost in his own need for Zach. His hand slipped between him and the bed, and his hips angled upward to give himself room. The emotions that entangled his being with Night fueled the desire flowing through Zach body like fire.

The tension became stronger and stronger as his fingers flew over the hardness of his cock. Thankfully, his pillow silenced Zach's pained cry when release eluded him. He wanted his vampire lover so badly it hurt. Fueling the fantasy in his head, it was the vivid image of Night's face that finally sent him over the edge. His mind screamed the vampire's name repeatedly until his tears wet the pillow.

Chapter 15

Markus had tried to talk them out of going
back, but between Kat, Harriet, and Zach, he'd soon
learned the futility of doing so. It had only taken them
a day to reach the border between Terrasan and
Night's domain.

Their ride had been uneventful until Zach
spotted a banner flying over a series of tents camped
on the Terrasan side of the border. Realizing the group
of resistance fighters probably patrolled the border,
Zach reined in the horse and led him off the main road.

"What's wrong, Zach?"

"Those men are resistance fighters, Kat. From
Callahan's army. And they aren't the most scrupulous
out there. It's not likely they will let us pass into Dark
Territory."

"But why would it matter to them that we are
going to Night's domain?"

"Kat, most of the resistance fighters only try to
stop the caravans of yearly allotments from leaving
Terrasan. But there are some who would kill anyone
who associated with the vampires. Callahan's men
wouldn't hesitate to kill us."

When they came to a riverbank, Zach directed
his horse to follow along the shoreline. They weren't
that damn far from Night's domain. It would have
been easier to use the main road, but there was more
than one way to get there.

"Why doesn't the seat of Terrasan stop them?"

"Why don't they stop any of it, Kat? Some Zh'dhat are afraid of angering the vampires and some are secretly funding those like Callahan while they pretend to be afraid of the vampires. If the Dominions of the Dark Territory manage to catch up with Callahan or the ones like him, the Zh'dhat that pay them money remain safe in their elite perches."

Confused, Kat muttered, "Their governing seat makes no sense."

They rode on in silence until Zach judged they were far enough away from Callahan's encampment. Veering away from the river, they made their way through the trees towards Night's land.

Even after they crossed, Zach didn't relax. He'd heard far too much about Callahan's methods to relax until they were closer to Night's mansion. An odd whistling sound through the trees alerted Zach to trouble, and he yelled, "Run, Kat."

Before she could react, an arrow embedded in the right flank of her horse, and the animal reared in pain. Kat was able to jump free before the horse came down and took off headlong into the forest.

Several men approached them on horseback. "What do we have here? Terrasans mistakenly on the wrong side of the border or vampire toys?"

"Does it matter? Just kill them, Saul." A bored drawl answered him.

Zach leaned over to scoop up his sister and placed her in front of him. He would be able to use his body as a shield to protect his sister long enough to get away from them.

A loud bellow roared through the suddenly still air. "Who dares trespass on Dominion Night's domain?"

To Zach's relief, Lotra and a small command of vampires appeared at the top of the hill to the west. Behind him he heard the hasty retreat of the men who had accosted them.

Several vampires broke off from the squadron to chase the retreating horsemen as Lotra approached Zach and Kat. They could see the astonished confusion on the commander's features as he approached them. "What are you two doing here?"

"We're coming home, Lotra." Kat gave him an impish grin before she climbed down from Zach's horse and ran over to the vampire.

With a great burst of laughter, the commander reached down, encircling her waist with his arm, then drew her up. Settling her in front of him, Lotra waited for the rest of his men to return.

When they came back, they were empty-handed. "They reached the border before we could catch them, Commander."

"They are camped near the main road, Lotra. Obviously, they've set themselves to patrol the border." Zach filled Lotra in on what he knew. "It's Callahan's men, and they don't have good reputations among the resistance fighters."

"Ah, that sort." Turning to one of his men, Lotra issued his orders. "I want two squads out here to keep an eye on them. Have Orpheus message Dominion Night and the Imperial Command about the main road."

* * *

"Kat and Zach have just arrived, Orpheus. What do you want me to do?"

"What?" Astonished, Opheus blinked at him, unsure if he'd heard him right.

Aggravated, Lotra scowled at him. "Kat and Zach are waiting in the front hall to see Dominion Night. What should I do?"

Quickly standing, Orpheus motioned him away. "I'll take care of it."

Lotra made himself scarce, heading back down to his office. Striding down the hall, Orpheus grabbed one of the servants, issuing orders. "Have Kat and Zach's old rooms prepared immediately."

With a bob of her head, the young girl scurried off to take care of the matter. Continuing down the hall, Orpheus wasn't sure what to think. Had the little minx talked her brother into returning? A smile wreathed his lips. He had no doubt she had, and he'd missed the young girl.

When he emerged from the back hall into the main entry, the first thing he heard was Kat shrieking his name before a body flew across the hall and collided with him. Enveloping her in a tight hug, Orpheus picked her up off the ground. "Well, what do I have here?"

Laughter rumbled from his chest as she hugged

him. "I missed you, Orpheus. Where's Night?"

"He's at The Peak. He's been there since both of you left." Orpheus noted the flush staining Zach's cheeks.

"Can you take me there?"

"That would depend on why you want to see him, Zach."

At first Zach refused to meet the gaze pinned on him. He saw Kat's nod of encouragement, then Zach cleared his throat and finally said, "I need to see him. To talk to him."

"Is it that hard to tell me why? How do you expect to convince Night if you can't even speak of what you feel? Emotions between humans and vampires aren't unheard of, young Zach. It's not acceptable in your world, and to some it's not acceptable in mine. But if you're strong enough, you will make your own place. Both in this world and in his heart."

"I love him, Orpheus. I don't care what my world thinks, neither Kat nor I belong there anymore. Kat told me she believes Night feels the same toward me. I don't know if he does or not, but there is something between us."

A wry smile twisted Orpheus' lips. "She is right. Little though Night will admit it. He left very shortly after you two did, and he's not entirely happy at the Peak."

"Then you will take me to him?" He knew if he had to, he would go by himself, but things would be far easier if Orpheus helped him.

In answer, Orpheus turned and addressed the closest servant. "Tell Lostra I want two of the fastest horses saddled and have cook prepared a pack for Zach."

Kat laughed as she gleefully hugged her brother. Wrapping her in his tight embrace, Zach threw Orpheus a relieved look over his sister's shoulder.

* * *

Zach had never traveled through the Dark Territory, but it was now to be his world. He rode beside Orpheus on the road to The Peak, passing through the small villages and towns along the way.

Once they'd left Night's domain, he noticed the condition and treatment of humans varied. As they slowed their horses to enter another town, Orpheus commented, "Our world is now divided. Between those who would keep humans as slaves and those who believe the two can co-exist. The Imperial Command believes the latter. As do Dominion Night and his Elder."

"Can both worlds live together?" Zach asked quietly as they traversed the quiet street. He knew there was a great deal for him to learn.

"If the law remains as it is and if Terrasan more strongly regulates the yearly allotments, I think they can. On both sides there are too many abuses. It's not just the vampires." Once outside the town, Orpheus gestured to a small path that led off the road. "We will stop here to eat and rest."

Zach guided his horse to follow Orpheus then slid out of the saddle. Opening the pack, he pulled out a cloth covered bundle. "The yearly allotment should be abolished."

"Not abolished but protected. Some of the cities far to the south allow their own citizens to choose among themselves. It is the practice of those who use the allotments to rid themselves of enemies or to steal another's property that should be abolished."

He settled beside Orpheus under the shade of the towering trees and opened his bundle. "I know some of my people use the excuse of allotments to gain power. It's part of what the resistance fights. But what cities let the people choose?"

"Dominion Night's Elder, Tern, works with Reison and Terra Cap. He very closely governs the allotments and placements. Night's progeny, Uyla, has just been given a command position. She will be working with Vernal and the lower seat of Second Land in the same manner."

"I still don't understand why some would choose to come here, Orpheus."

"Some have no home and no chance where they are and do willingly choose to come here. Dominion Tern insures they are placed with other Dominions who will treat them fairly."

"You mean like Night?"

"Dominion Night accepts humans from others who are not so nice or strict in their own rules. He already knows his Elder will see to the care of those he is responsible for." Orpheus leaned back against the tree behind him, closing his eyes.

Zach considered the information he'd been given. Even the gruff, red-headed vampire beside him treated humans with a certain amount of respect.

If things hadn't been different in Night's domain, Zach would have never returned. But he'd never realized just how different Night's ways were. Nor that it extended to Night's family. Given what he knew of Night's temperament, he wasn't surprised though.

Silently, Zach ate his small meal then drank some water from the pouch. The only thing that worried him about his decision to return to Night was how Night would react. Kat seemed to think Night loved him, but Zach wasn't so sure of that. Zach just couldn't forget what had happened between them, and he realized he never would. In some way he felt he belonged to Night. As if the two of them were tied together in some strange way.

Closing his eyes, he rested back against the tree. Although he had done his best to ignore the indefinable force that seemed to draw him to Night, he never fully succeeded. No one knew how much it had hurt him to leave Night in the first place. Now he needed to convince Night to let him stay.

A great deal of uncertainty centered on Night's reaction. He had no clue what the vampire would say or do. Was he risking all for nothing? Those doubts plagued him, and not for the first time Zach was tempted to turn around and run. What if? His thoughts whispered incessantly to him.

Zach's eyes flew open and saw Orpheus' green eyes trained on him, a faint look of sympathy within them.

When the doors at the far end of the hall opened, several heads turned toward the newcomers. Whispers began drifting through the crowd as Orpheus strode into the room. When they reached the dais where Night and Bran lounged, the group parted.

"Perhaps I was forgotten after all."

Night had paid no attention to the sounds in the room until he heard the familiar voice. He froze for an instant in disbelief before he pulled slowly from Bran and looked up to see Zach standing over them. "What are you doing here?"

Zach's gaze narrowed on Bran, and he drew a deep breath, fighting the instantaneous surge of jealousy. A flicker of amusement appeared on Bran's features as he smilingly studied Zach. Night stood slowly, blocking Zach's view of the other vampire.

Orpheus shrugged when Night looked quickly at him. "He wanted me to bring him to The Peak."

"A long story," Zach said simply. "Can we speak…" He looked around. "…in private?"

For the first time in his existence, Night was disconcerted. Bran gave him an amused look but said nothing as he reached for his wine. With a nod, Night took hold of Zach's arm. Drawing him out of the public rooms, he ignored the high interest of the others present.

He led go of Zach and led him down several corridors without saying a word until they reached his private quarters. Opening the door, Night gestured for Zach to enter.

Zach walked into the room and turned, waiting silently as Night closed the door.

Leaning against the door, Night didn't say anything right away. His gaze trailed over Zach slowly, drinking in the sight of him. When he spoke, his voice held a quietly calm note that he didn't quite feel. "Why are you here, Zach?"

Whatever Night felt, Zach couldn't read him. Stepping toward him, Zach laid his hand on Night's chest. "We tried to stay in the village, but neither of us were happy there."

"Kat is here as well?"

"She stayed at your house, and I came here with Orpheus." How could he explain to Night what he felt? He couldn't even tell if Night was happy to see him.

He glanced down at Zach's hand on his chest then raised his eyes to meet Zach's gaze. "Why?"

Pulling in a deep breath, Zach tried his best to answer the question. "Because I can't live without you. I don't want to live without you."

A brief glimmer of pain reflected in Night's eyes before it vanished. "It will fade in time, Zach. You bonded yourself to me without realizing it, but it's not permanent."

"No, you're wrong." Indignation twisted Zach features as his finger poked Night. "I might have never been in love until I met you, but I know what it feels like it.

"By coming here, you have made it impossible to return to Terrasan." Night gently removed Zach's hand from his chest then released it. "You have no other choice but to remain here. I am not happy that you've chosen to do this, Zach. My world is not your world."

"It will be. That's why I'm here." Shaking his head vehemently, Zach stepped abruptly back from him. "I understand you and your world better than you think I do, Night."

"I want you to remain in this room until Orpheus brings you some clothes. You will need to wear the colors of my house so that none of the others here will bother you. What's done is done. I will do my best to make your life as comfortable as possible."

The formal tone of Night's voice dismayed Zach, and he could find no sign of any real emotion on the vampire's face. When Night turned, Zach took a step forward, but Night didn't pause. Before the door closed behind Night, Zach had to say one more thing. "I love you, Night."

He knew Night had heard him, but the door still closed. Frustrated, Zach strode to the bed and threw himself on it. He already realized it wouldn't be easy, but he'd expected Night would at least hear him out.

"Impossible bastard." Muttering, Zach smacked the pillow. No matter what it took, he would convince Night they belonged together. Just knowing Night was somewhere near had eased a great deal of the restlessness within Zach.

* * *

Bran watched his friend pace restlessly back and forth in front of him. Nothing had been said about what was bothering the vampire, and Bran waited for Night to explain. Smirking faintly, his gaze followed Night. As the moments passed Night's movements seem to become more agitated, and finally Bran asked outright, "You didn't expect the young man to come here, did you?"

"No." Answering tersely, Night's attempt to rein in his dismay and temper failed abysmally. "How could they? They were both safe in their village. Why would Zach and Kat return here?"

"I would suspect because they both love you. In their own ways."

Night stopped abruptly, staring at him blankly. "I believe that of Kat. No doubt she convinced her brother to return here. But Zach hates me, he hates all vampires."

"Apparently not." Bran murmured under his breath.

"Anything else is nothing more than the bonding. It should never have happened, and it will fade."

"Ah, but that still doesn't explain your love for him. It may also be true in Zach's case." Bran tried to pin his friend down with implacable logic, and Night knew exactly what he was trying to do.

"My heart beats in rhythm to his," Night finally admitted. "But I never hated the young man. Not as he hates me. He blames me for the death of his mother and kidnapping Kat."

"And now he knows who was to blame. In mortals hate is very akin to love."

"I never would have condemned them to a lifetime in this world, Bran. Not with things so precarious."

"I know that. But you have no choice. To send them back to Terrasan would be disastrous for both of them. They would at minimum be completely rejected. At worst, they will be killed."

"They will remain with me, but I have no desire to subject Zach to those here." With an impatient motion, Night sat on the ledge of the fountain.

"You will return home?"

"Unfortunately, I can't. Not right now. Will you watch over him when I'm in session with Tere?"

Before Bran could answer, Uyla hurried across the garden, approaching them. One of her servants followed quickly after her.

"Is it true, my elder?" A faint smile hovered over her lips as she eyed Night.

"Is what true, Uyla?"

"I've heard Orpheus brought a young mortal to see you."

With a repressive air, Night answered her. "Yes, Zach is here."

A look passed between her and Bran. Night

didn't miss it and frowned severely.

Laughing softly, Uyla leaned down, draping her arms over Night's shoulders and pressed a kiss to his forehead. "I wondered how you would react if your young mortal decided to challenge your outdated beliefs."

"Uyla," he started warningly, but the light touch of her finger to his lips silenced him.

"You need to be shaken from your misguided notions. So don't argue with me, dearest. You know I'm right."

Bran did his best to try to hide his amusement, but one look at Night's face had him laughing. "She's right, you know."

The young servant hovered nearby, shifting slightly as he waited for his mistress.

"You've taken in someone new, I see." Night addressed Uyla, hoping to change the subject.

Clearly, she would have none of it. "You aren't going to send Zach back, are you?"

"No, I am not sending him back. I will take care of Zach and Kat as I do all of my mortals."

"Night." Uyla pinched at his arm in exasperation. "The young man obviously loves you. He risked a great deal to come back to you."

When Night looked to Bran for a little help, his best friend shrugged.

"You know you love him as well."

At her words, Night abruptly stood and walked off. He could still hear their conversation as he headed toward the main meeting chamber.

"He's being stubborn, Bran."

"Give him some time, Uyla. I have no doubt young Zach will be able to wear away that resistance."

With an impatient snap, Night shut the door, blocking them out. Neither of them seemed to understand the impossibility of a relationship between him and Zach. It didn't help matters that Night's senses could too easily pick up Zach's whereabouts.

For a moment he allowed himself to remember the sweet feel of Zach's warm body. His hands clenched in fists at his sides as he struggled with the sudden surge of need to be close to Zach.

Night had heard the words Zach had whispered to him before he left him. In that brief second, Night hadn't been able to control the leap of hope that filled him. Silently, he made his way past the others who were lounging at their leisure in the banquet hall. There was only one place Night would find the peace and quiet he craved.

The Imperial's temple was a place very few Dominions entered. Passing through the enormous archway, Night welcomed complete quiet in the cavernous room. Row after row of tiered candles lit the darkness, the light of their flames dancing over the surface of the gleaming red and white stone walls.

He sat on one of the white marble benches, staring at the serene faces of his god. The two faces of Eimmen gazed down on him, and Night was grateful for the calming sense sweeping through him. His faith in his world and in the natural order had never been shaken. Yet, he wasn't at all certain of himself anymore.

The feelings inside him confused him even more because they hadn't faded as he'd expected they would. Zach had turned Night inside out by returning. The only thing that could account for the reversal of Zach's feelings was the artificial bond of Night's blood. He just doubted he could get Zach to understand that.

Sighing, he remained pensive, trying to guard his wayward thoughts from dwelling on memories of Zach and him together.

* * *

"I have some news from one of Counselor Uyla's servants that may interest you."

"What, Qurfar?" Orshan grunted as he set his glass on the table nearby.

"I'll let the servant explain." He gestured to the cowering mortal nearby then scowled when the young man hesitated.

"I o-overheard them talking." His hands clenched nervously in front of him as he stopped in front of Orshan.

"Yes, yes, get on with it." Orshan snapped impatiently.

Swallowing convulsively, the servant nodded. "The mortal, Zach, came here because he's in love with Dominion Night. I heard them talking to Dominion Night about him being in love with the mortal as well."

"Night in love with a human?" A glint of

interest appeared in Orshan's eyes as they rested on Qurfar. "I think we can put this to good use."

"I thought it might be useful to you." After he bowed to Orshan, Quafar grabbed the servant's arm in a bruising grip. "Now return to your position, Kal, or it will be the worse for you."

When Quafar released him, Kal ran from the room.

Chapter 17

Zach sat on the edge of the bed, moodily picking at the covers. He'd scarcely seen Night lately and realized the vampire was avoiding him. Even though it probably wasn't a wise idea to leave the room, Zach was damn close to being tempted to do so. If only to find Night.

Hearing a light knock at the door, Zach's heart started racing as he jumped off the bed and ran to answer it. Maybe Night had finally come to his senses. When he opened it and saw Bran standing there, the momentary giddiness faded. "Oh… it's you. If you want Night, he's not here."

"Actually, I came to talk to you." Bran gave him a slight smile. "May I come in?"

"Me?" Staring in confusion at the vampire, Zach hesitated for a long moment before he remembered to open the door further and let Bran in. "What do you want with me?"

Bran shrugged as he stepped into the room. He looked around for a moment, then back at Zach. "To talk?"

Zach disliked the vampire in front of him with a passion, yet he tried to control that. Closing the door behind him, Zach headed back to the bed and sat stiffly at the edge. "Talk about what? Looks to me like Night prefers your company over mind. So if you're worried, don't be."

Sighing dramatically, Bran sat down in one of

the two chairs near the hearth. "Zach. Honestly. Do you think there is any emotion there between me and Night?" Before Zach could say a word, Bran continued. "We play. That's it. But with you… Well, let's just say that Night sees in you, much more than he sees in anyone."

Conflicted about the message Bran was trying to send him, Zach wasn't so sure if he believed him. "Yeah, right. That's why he's been hanging around me ever since I got here. He can't seem to get enough of me."

Bran smirked and sat back, looking quite at home. "Night is… a busy man. Perhaps he just needs someone to remind him of what's important now and then? Just smack him on the head a few times, threaten to leave, and he'll drop to one knee and declare his love. He's a stubborn old mule, Zach."

For the first time a glimmer of hope ignited in Zach. He'd almost lost heart because he hadn't seen Night at all, not after his admission of his own love to Night. Now he started to wonder if it was because Night was avoiding his own feelings. "Is that why he won't come to see me? I thought he just didn't want anything to do with me."

Bran snorted. "Hard to believe that the big-bad Dominion is terrified of falling in love?"

Eyeing the vampire with a consider look, Zach quipped dryly, "You're enjoying this, aren't you? I thought the two of you were together. I mean, you both looked pretty well wrapped up in each other when I first got here."

"I'm enjoying myself immensely, especially if it means I get to watch Night squirm. As for us… Sex and feeding. That's all it's ever been between us. I respect him, he respects me. But there is no love between us, Zach."

"I find that hard to believe. Do you plan on continuing the uh, sex and feeding?" The question came out with a belligerent edge.

"Believe what you will," Bran said with a shrug. "I know my heart and I know Night. You have him wrapped around your finger, whether you realize it or not. As for the feeding and sex…" Bran sat forward in the chair, gaze pinned on Zach. "We haven't done anything since you returned."

Zach stared searchingly at Bran, trying to decipher the truth. It was hard for him to believe that the two had no feelings for each other, but there would be no reason for Bran to say otherwise, unless it was true. "Then he's not around you all time? He's just avoiding me."

"Not around me at all," Bran corrected. "And he's not so much avoiding you… as he is avoiding the inevitable truth: he's in love with you, and it scares the hell out of him."

"I hadn't thought of that." Zach lip's twitched into a devious smile. "Now I just need to figure out how to corner him."

"He's in his office," Bran said with a wink. "Last I heard, he had a few letters to write. I'm sure he needs a break."

"Yeah, but will he stay put to hear me out?" The smile faded into a troubled expression. "Last time he just walked out."

"If you believe it will be a problem, I'll just have to make sure he can't."

Zach had a few qualms about that. But he realized it wasn't likely Night would hear him out without a little extra help. Sighing quietly, he nodded his head in agreement.

"You'll also want to meet Uyla. She's Night only daughter and a Counsel for the Imperial command. I'm fairly sure she is most impatiently curbing her curiosity about you.

"Is that good or bad?" Zach wasn't sure if she would be hostile or friendly toward him.

"Oh, she's quite delighted that Night has finally met his match, Zach. You've no need to worry about her. Just give me time to arrange everything with Night, and I'll return after everything is ready."

As Bran stood, Zach said, "Thank you for being so willing to help."

"I'm just as delighted as Uyla is about all of this." After flashing Zach a wicked grin, Bran left the room.

* * *

Zach paced anxiously in Bran's quarters. The vampire had told him he'd send Night there and to just wait for him. That wasn't so easy to do. A million what ifs raced through Zach's thoughts. He wasn't sure how he would handle it if Night absolutely refused to listen to him.

The only other choice he had was to return to Night's domain. Zach didn't think he'd be able to handle remaining here if Night completely rejected him. In his mind, he nearly had himself half packed before he heard the sound of the doorknob turning.

He stopped abruptly and waited for Night to enter, his heart racing enough to leave him light-headed.

Night came in and shut the door behind him before he saw Zach. "What are you doing here?"

"We have to talk, Night." Zach tried to hide his own fear behind a calm mask.

"About?"

Finding himself the recipient of Night's suspicious gaze, Zach swallowed against the tightness of his own throat. "Us. How I feel about you."

Night turned to open the door and found it won't budge. With a frustrated growl, he pulled harder and still it wouldn't open.

"Bran made sure you would stay to listen to me, Night."

Spinning around, Night made a concerted effort to subdue the agitation rising in him. "Whatever feelings you have aren't your own. You know that as well as I."

"I know no such thing, Night." Zach remained where he was for the moment, not daring to get closer to the vampire. They needed to talk, and Zach knew he wouldn't be talking if he were near Night. "I did drink your blood, but it started way before that. I'm not sure you'll ever understand."

Caught off guard by the pronouncement, Night leaned against the door. His own tangled emotions were impossible to sort though. He knew he should leave, but the near hopeless look on Zach's face stilled him.

"I just wanted to talk, Night. To explain. Whether or not I'm supposed to, I already love you. I couldn't forget about you even when we returned to the village. Now I don't want to forget you, I want to be with you."

"You shouldn't have come back, Zach." The words were only a half-hearted protest. Night couldn't even kid himself. Deep inside he was overjoyed Zach had come back to him. "I don't understand why you did."

Instead of answering, Zach approached him slowly. Placing his hands on either side of Night's head, palms flat against the door, Zach stood close enough that Night could feel the heat of his breath. "For you," Zach whispered. Without giving Night a chance to answer, Zach leaned in and kissed him, tongue pushing into Night's mouth.

Initially surprised, Night didn't react right away but a moment later, he slipped his arms around Zach, pulling him as close as he could, giving into the kiss. It had been too long since he'd held Zach in his arms. The surprise wore off and Night became more aggressive, unable to suppress any of the feelings welling inside him. His hands caressed down Zach's back to his ass, and his tongue pushed back against Zach, seeking the taste of his mouth.

Zach reached for Night, hips grinding against him as Zach fucked Night's mouth with his tongue, sliding it under one fang, nicking it. The taste of his blood tinged their kiss, and Zach groaned, pushing against Night and pinning him to the door.

Night tried his damnedest to pull his senses back together. The taste of Zach's blood only sent a sharp surge of hunger through him, and he barely bit back his own growl as he broke off the kiss. "Zach. You hate me."

"And I tried for three months to convince myself of that." Zach wouldn't budge. "I tried to forget you, Night. It didn't work. The harder I tried, the more I wanted you."

"Are you so sure you mean that?" His hands remained where he'd placed them though he knew he should probably let go of Zach.

"More than I think you realize. I'm not leaving, Night."

Night didn't know what to say to him. Several things went through his mind, but they all remained unsaid. Gently touching his face, he asked softly, "What makes you think I really wanted you to go in the first place?"

"If you didn't, then why did you send me home?"

"It's where you and Kat belong, and where I thought you wanted to be."

"I belong here," Zach whispered. He leaned in and licked Night's lips. "With you."

Night captured his tongue, silencing both of them. The mood that had haunted him since Zach left faded and he began to relax. The press of Zach's body told him how much his lover had missed him and wanted him.

Zach lowered his hands, fingers working Night's pants open. "Want to taste you," he whispered on Night's lips. "Missed this." Zach's hand curled around Night's cock, stroking slowly. "Missed you."

A groan escaped Night with the feel of Zach's hand around him. Night had absolutely no resistance to him. After getting rid of his shoes and pants quickly, a push of his hand to Zach's shoulder edged him toward the bed.

Zach walked backward to the bed, stripping as he went. By the time he tumbled back into the bed, he was completely naked and couldn't stop the surge of need rushing through him. His gaze lingered on Night as the vampire undressed then stood at the edge of the bed.

"There will be no going back, Zach, not after this. Make no mistake. You've given yourself to me, and you belong to me." Night hesitated, giving Zach one last chance to get the hell out.

"Just shut up and get over here." Zach muttered, stretching sensually against the cover.

Night obliged him, sliding to the bed to hover over Zach. A nudge of his knees parted Zach's legs, and Night's gaze roamed over the delectable sight of Zach spread out for him. Taking Zach's cock in hand, the ball of Night's thumb rubbed against the slit.

A smile of appreciation curled Night's lips as Zach reacted instantly. A low moan rose in Zach's throat, and his hand covered Night. "Not enough. More. I want more."

After releasing Zach, Night prepared himself using the small bottle of oil kept near the bed. Once he was slicked, he lowered his hand, fingers pushing between the cheeks of Zach's ass.

Zach instantly grabbed his legs and brought them up, opening himself to Night. A soft whimper sounded from him when Night's fingers pushed into him. A slow twist smeared Zach's passage with the oil then probed deeper, leaving Zach panting heavily.

The heated flare of Night's eyes revealed how close Night was to losing it. His gaze met Zach's before he pulled back his hand, and his body pinned Zach's to the bed. In eagerness, Zach wrapped his legs around Night, trying to force Night inside him.

"So anxious for me." A satisfied purr laced through the words, and Night's lips covered Zach's, his tongue hungrily seeking entry. Before Zach could react, Night slowly filled him. With the exquisite stretch of heat and sensation around his cock, Night pushed more forcefully, and Zach rocked as hard as he could, encouraging the vampire.

Night was caught in the sweet feelings pulsing straight from his cock to his brain. The beautiful sound of Zach's moan and the claw of Zach's nails on his back sent Night's desire soaring. He rode the undulation of Zach's body frantically seeking its own release.

Ending the kiss, Night lifted his head and a triumphant growl rumbled from him as he watched his young lover go over the edge. Zach's features became taut with the inner pleasure and his body strained to Night, writhing desperately.

Before Zach could come down, Night struck swiftly, burying his fangs in Zach's throat and his cock in Zach's ass. The sudden flood rushed through him, leaving him shuddering in its wake as Zach's blood spilled in his mouth.

Chapter 18

Zach had been literally floating in the clouds since Night left to attend one of the Imperial command meetings. Bunching the covers beneath his hands, he stretched lazily, savoring each small ache of his body. He knew, without doubt, he was exactly where he belonged.

When a knock sounded at the door, Zach grabbed for Night's robe and slipped it on as he scooted off the bed. When he opened the door, he saw one of Uyla's servants. "Night's already in the Imperial command meeting."

"I'm Kal. Counselor Uyla asked me to bring you to her quarters." After bowing politely to Zach, he stepped back and waited.

Zach knew Uyla was Night's daughter, and he wasn't surprised she wanted to meet him. He was just as eager to meet her. "Let me get dressed and I'll be right out."

Zach closed the door then stripped out of the robe. As quickly as he could, he washed up at the basin then got dressed. Oddly, it gave him a sense of pride to wear Night's colors.

No more than a few moments passed before Zach reopened the door and stepped into the hall. Kal led the way down the corridor and up a set of stairs. Zach followed him, his thoughts preoccupied with Night. After a series of turns in the maze of corridors, Kal stopped and opened one of the doors. He gestured for Zach to enter as he held the door open.

Zach gave him a friendly nod before he stepped inside. Nobody was in the room, and when Kal shut the door, Zach turned to look back at him to ask where Uyla was. Surprised to see Kal hadn't come in, Zach glanced around the room to find a place to sit. The walls were devoid of any decorations and seemed stark compared to Night's rooms.

There were three closed doors and Zach debated about knocking at one but then stilled when one of the doors opened. "Ah, Zachary Bern, I've heard a great deal about you."

Zach nodded politely, uncertain who the guy was. A sudden dizzy feeling swamped Zach, and he stumbled back before reaching for the wall behind him.

"Don't worry, young Zach. You'll be well taken care of until Night gives me what I want."

The vampire's voice sounded distant as Zach slid down the wall then collapsed on the floor.

* * *

Zach opened his eyes, confused by the dreary grayness surrounding him. Incomprehensible shapes danced in his vision before it slowly began to clear. The first thing he saw was the grinning face of a man. It took him a second to remember what might have happened, then Zach bolted upright.

"You're not going anywhere, Zach. So you may as well enjoy your stay here." Unperturbed, the vampire continued watching him.

"Who are you? What's going on?"

"I am Orshan. And you are my guest until further notice." An unpleasant smile crossed his lips at Zach's look of alarm. "I see you've at least heard my name."

Trying to still his panicked thoughts, Zach glanced wildly around for any escape route. When Zach looked about to bolt, Orshan spoke again, "It won't do you any good to escape, young Zach. You don't even know where you are. We're a good distance from The Peak, and Night isn't going to be rushing to your rescue any time soon."

A servant came into the room with a small plate of food. He set it beside the bed then stepped back.

"Since I never waste good food on the likes of mortals, you better enjoy your meal. You'll not have another until tomorrow." Orshan stood then gestured for the servant to follow him.

"Night will kill you." Zach shot back before the door closed behind the two. He didn't give a damn where he was. Ignoring the food, Zach stood and hurried toward the door. Waiting for a short time just to insure the two men were gone, he finally opened the door and peered out.

Not hearing any sound, Zach stepped out into the corridor. From the drab appearance of the area, he assumed he was in the servant's quarters. Zach had heard stories from his sister and Night about how Orshan tried his mortals. It'd been enough to make Zach's skin crawl.

He had to get out of here. Somehow, he would

find a way back to Night once he got outside. Zach heard the low murmur of voices before he saw the other three servants. He froze immediately, but none of them paid any attention to him. Emboldened, Zach walked past them.

No one tried to stop him, and Zach relaxed slightly. He could smell the scent of cut hay and followed it, hoping it would lead him outside. Further down the hall a door opened, and Zach caught the flash of sunshine before the door shut behind a young woman. He hastened his step, though tried not to break out into a desperate run.

Yanking the door open, he stepped through it and found himself not too far away from a field of partially harvested hay. The woman was drawing water from a pump nearby. She gave him no more than a cursory glance before she went back to her task.

Zach dashed across the open area and into the hay, heading for the line of trees at the back of the field. Nothing looked familiar to him, but as long as he kept going, he was sure he would be all right.

Alert to any sounds of a chase behind him, Zach fled into the forest, trying to keep his panic from slipping free. He knew Orshan would be able to get anything he wanted out of Night as long as Zach was his captive. Zach already knew exactly what Orshan wanted. He also knew Night would give it to him just to get Zach back.

Zach slowed on the rising incline of the ground. Up ahead, he could see the top of a hill higher than the surrounding trees. He headed straight for it, hoping it would give him an idea of where he was. As the trees thinned, the sun shone down on his head, warming him enough to make him sweat. He could hear no other sounds but the chatter of birds within the trees.

When he reached the top, his heart sank as he slowly turned completely around. There was nothing but trees in every direction. The only other thing he saw was Orshan's buildings in a large clearing. There was absolutely nothing else but trees and sky.

He knew Night's domain bordered Orshan's in the direction of Terrasan. If he kept his back to the sun, he would head in the general direction of Night's castle. Sighing heavily, he glanced back at the buildings. It meant going back in the direction he came, but he planned on giving Orshan's compound a wide berth.

* * *

When Night could detect no trace of Zach within the confines of the city, he summoned his elder and daughter. Uyla had gone straight to the Imperial command, and Tere had sent his servants to begin searching for Zach outside the city gates.

Agitated, Night paced rapidly back and forth. In another desperate attempt, he expanded his senses, sending his power out in all directions. He fiercely focused on finding any small hint of Zach then abruptly stopped the useless endeavor when he found no sign of his lover. Wherever Zach was, he wasn't in The Peak.

He strode angrily to the door then had to stop when it opened. When he saw Orshan's smirking face, Night clenched his fists at his side.

"I've heard you lost something, Night."

"I should have known," Night snarled before lunging at Orshan.

With a laugh, Orshan stood his ground. "Harm me and you'll never find him. I guarantee that."

The words brought Night up short. Barely stifling his growl of outrage, Night glared at him. "Return him to me or I will kill you."

"He'll be returned to you as soon as you favor my new petition for an increase in the allotment of mortals, Night. It's that simple. Give me what I want, and I will give you what you want."

"Where is he, Orshan?" Night took a threatening step forward then grabbed Orshan by the collar of his tunic. "If you harm him in any way not even the Imperial command can stop me from tearing you apart."

"It won't do you any good to know where he is, but I will tell you anyway. He was in my keep."

Night pushed him to the side then abruptly released him. Before Night could make it to the door, Orshan said, "If you plan on going there, be aware that Zach has escaped. Of course, the young man didn't realize that's exactly what I wanted him to do. My domain is nearly as vast as yours, Night. You'll never find him in time. Not before I get to him."

Night froze and slowly turned to face Orshan.

Before he could say anything, Orshan added, "It will do you no good to go to the Imperial command. I will only tell Tersus that I took advantage of the opportunity and had nothing to do with Zach's disappearance. You have no proof I am involved in this."

"You're a fool, Orshan, for risking your life just for the sake of getting a few more mortals. If Zach isn't returned to me, you'll die."

With a smug expression, Orshan folded his arms across his chest. "I have every intention of returning the young mortal to you, Night. I'm not terribly worried about the risk. I'm also fairly sure you'll manage to convince Zach to never reveal my name."

It was the only thing that stilled Night's blood thirsty desire to drain Orshan. He knew Orshan had him right where the other vampire wanted him. While Night's powers were strong, he wouldn't be able to immediately find Zach in Orshan's domain. The moment Night set foot in Orshan's domain, Orshan would know it.

"You've won." Night growled out. "For now, but watch your back, Orshan. If you don't bring him back to me, I'll hunt you down. There will be nothing left of you if anything happens to Zach."

Reaching for the door, Orshan paused and smirked at him. "Oh, I promise you'll have him back in one piece as soon as I have my vote."

Night knew what Orshan's promises were

worth, but in this case, he knew the vampire would return Zach. To do otherwise would mean death.

After Orshan left, Night still considered ideas and discarded them just as ready. If Zach had remained at Orshan's keep, the matter would have been a great deal easier. However, with no clue of where Zach might be in Orshan's domain, Night didn't dare risk the chance that he'd get to his lover before Orshan did. He had no real choice but to attend the Imperial command meeting and vote as Orshan wanted him to.

It went against everything Night believed in, but there wasn't a damn thing he could do about it.

Chapter 19

Climbing to the top of the ridge, Zach could no longer see Orshan's compound. There was nothing else around him but trees and more trees. Off to the left, he spotted a small clearing and the glint of water in the fading sunlight. The sun was already beginning to dip below the horizon, and he needed to find a place to camp for the night.

Trudging slowly down the hill, Zach headed for the clearing. He'd managed to get this far, but he wouldn't make it much further without food and water. His foster father had trained him well in surviving with next to little in the middle of nowhere.

When he reached the water's edge, he noticed an overabundance of green *thaylen*. Luck was now on his side. Zach crouched down, scooping up a handful of the water and drank it. He recognized the sweet taste as being from a deep spring and untainted. The gods were on his side as well.

Settling cross-legged near the water's edge, he reached for one of the smaller gourds. He had to twist the end several times before it opened. Using his finger, he scooped up some of the inside pulp and began eating it. Though it wasn't all that tasty, it would fill him up, and he could use the skins to carry water. Not knowing how far it was to Night's domain or how long it would take him, Zach would have to fill several gourds just in case.

After he finished with it, he put it in the water,

letting it fill up to wash away most of the sticky residue of the plant. Then he drained the water and set the gourd aside on the grass and picked another gourd. Night was already falling and soon the watering hole would probably draw more than one species of wild animal.

Zach quickly satisfied his hunger then picked up the washed gourds and stood to scout the surrounding area. He didn't want to camp too far from the pool, yet it had to be far enough away not to attract any of the animals who would stop at the clearing.

Stepping through the thicker underbrush, Zach walked for a few moments before he found the perfect tree. He laid the gourd skins on a low hanging branch then began shimmying up the wide trunk, using the knobs and thinner branches to hold to. When he saw a nest of branches close enough together, he inched himself onto them to test them holding his weight.

Small creaks of sound followed his movements, but the branches held, and Zach settled in for the night. He'd be far safer up here from prowling animals, and it was likely he would fall out in the middle of the night. Closing his eyes, he focused on thoughts on Night, and the mental image brought a prick of tears to his eyes. No matter what, he would find his way back to Night.

* * *

On the second day, Zach woke long before the sun rose and had decided to risk continuing on. The sun was already high in the sky when Zach stopped for a rest on an outcropping of rocks.

He scanned the land and caught a glimpse of a ribbon of water. Could it be the river bordering Night's domain? Zach ate part of a gourd and drank some water. Far too used to farm labor, he was at all tired yet. His thoughts lightened with the belief he might be close to Night's domain and didn't notice the ache of his feet quite so much.

Standing, he determinedly quickened his pace. If he reached the river in decent time and followed along the bank, he might be home before night fall.

The buzz of insects and warbling sounds of the birds accompanied Zach. High in the trees bright red sun birds called out in warning to one another as Zach walked beneath their trees. At this point, Zach absolutely refused to give up. The memory of Night kept him going.

A short time later, he reached the river and followed the placid waters, hoping to find the narrowest part to cross. The other side had to be Night's domain. There were no landmarks or anything else Zach could identify. Across the river looked to be the same as the side he was on. Zach still continued, traveling along the edge of the water until he spotted a downed tree spanning the river like a bridge. Zach made use of it then stopped on the other side long enough to climb one of the nearby tall trees.

In the distance, he saw a tall, gray column of stone and instantly recognized it. His triumphant shout rang out among the trees. Laughing, Zach quickly clamored down.

Night sat in one of the lower tier seats, impassively watching the others conversing around him. Nearby, Orshan chortled gleefully with his cohorts. The sound of Orshan's voice grated on every last nerve Night had.

The Imperial Command had yet to appear, and it was already past to start the meeting. One of the Imperial guards entered the chamber and strode to the center of the room. When he held up his hand, everyone fell silent.

"The Imperial Command will be delayed for a short time longer. Dominion Talfour will start the meeting, and the petitions will begin as soon as the Imperial Command arrives."

Night had been waiting anxiously for all of this to be over. The delay set his nerves even more on edge. As Dominion Talfour addressed more mundane business, Tere settled beside Night.

His elder muttered in a tone of disgust, "I see Orshan is ready to restate his petition."

Night gave him a tight smile but said nothing. Worry over Zach had made a serious mess of his thoughts. He could outright attack Orshan and be damned to the consequences, but it wouldn't return Zach to him. Night had already struggled more than once with the temptation to kill Orshan.

He could still vote down the petition and hope to all the gods that he could get to Zach before Orshan did, but the odds weren't heavily in his favor. Night wasn't willing to risk Zach's life on such a slim chance. Orshan knew he had Night exactly where he wanted him.

Zach had been missing for three days, and Night could barely contain himself from tearing the whole damn place apart.

When the Imperial Command finally joined them, Dominion Talfour stepped to the side as Tisus walked up the dais to his throne. Angling for the best position, several other Dominions, including Orshan, lined up to present their petitions.

Night shifted restlessly, and Tere gave him a questioning look as the proceedings started. He answered his elder with a slight shake of his head before he turned his attention to the floor of the chamber.

After the first vote approved Dominion Agva's petition to increase his border guards, Orhsan stepped in front of the Imperial Command. "I am petitioning the council to increase our allotted mortals from ten to thirty for the duration of two years. After that, I ask for a permanent increase to fifteen."

This was against everything Night believed in; everything he'd been taught. His mind still rebelled even as Tisus looked to the other Dominions and nodded, waiting for their decision.

Night scowled at Orshan before his expression smoothed and he slowly raised his hand, palm showing. The gasp of shock from his elder only hammered home what Night had done.

Orshan had gained two more votes, and his petition would pass. Triumphantly, he turned back to the Imperial Command, waiting for the decree.

Tisus stood and walked to the edge of the dais. "The petition has passed with a vote of fourteen to thirteen. As Imperial Command, I am overruling the petition."

"You can't do that!" Orshan shouted, stepping angrily toward Tisus.

Night sat slumped in seat, not knowing what to think. Others around him stood in support of Orshan. Tisus gestured to Orshan, and two Imperial guards walked down the steps to him. Flanking him, they grabbed Orshan's arms and pulled him up the dais. With another gesture from Tisus, guards went to the tiered seats and took hold of Night and Agva. A ripple of shock reverberated through the room, and the other Dominions froze. Something was seriously wrong.

"The rest of you will leave these chambers and not return until I send for you." The Imperial Command tersely addressed the other Dominions.

Whispering amongst themselves, everyone else hurriedly left the room. When it was once again silent, Tisus said, "Orshan, you will explain to me why two of my most loyal supporters have voted for your petition."

Before Orshan could open his mouth, Zach appeared from behind the Imperial Command throne. Night froze in shock then rushed toward Zach. When Night reached Zach, he enfolded his lover in his arms, burying his face to Zach's throat.

"Imperial Command," Dominion Agva spoke as he stepped forward. "Orshan is holding the mortal son of my companion as hostage. It is why I petitioned for an increase in my border guards and voted in his petition."

Orshan struggled against the guards who held him but wasn't strong enough to free himself. "Tisus, the vote passed, you can't rescind the petition!"

"But I did, and for reasons none will argue against." When Tisus finished speaking Uyla and Kal stepped out from behind the throne.

A deep breath took in the reassuring scent of his lover, and Night ignored those around him as Zach silently clung to him. The fear and anxiety that had held Night hostage melted away. For the moment, he didn't care how Zach had returned to him, he only cared that the young man was back in his arms.

"You threatened both Zach and Kal's lives, Orshan, to coerce my elder and Dominion Agva into voting in favor of your petition." Uyla took Kal to Agva then released his hand, turning on Orshan again. "You deliberately put Kal in my household in the hopes that you would find something you could use against Night."

Blustering, Orshan's voice tone rose in threat, but Titus ignored him. "Take him downstairs."

As they took Orshan away, Tisus added, "You will remain under Imperial arrest until we can properly convene to address your treachery."

Zach glanced over at Tisus, giving him a grateful look as Night released him.

"I must apologize, Imperial Command…" Before Night could continue, Tisus held up his hand.

"I understand, Night. It is Orshan who will pay the price for his schemes." He waved them away with an indolent gesture. "I suggest you make yourselves scarce before I call the other Dominions back."

Uyla lightly patted Night's arm. "Go ahead, Night. I'll talk to Tere, and we will discuss why you didn't come to me tomorrow."

Night slipped his arm around Zach, drawing his lover with him and left. As they walked down the hall toward Night's quarter, Night eyed him. "You'll have to explain to me how you freed yourself. And how the Imperial Command became involved."

Shooting him a mischievous grin, Zach's arm snaked around Night. "It's really easy. I made it back to your domain, and Lotra brought me to The Peak. I didn't think it would do any good to just come to you. After I explained everything to the Imperial Command, he said he would watch the vote. If you did vote for Orshan's petition, it would be all the proof that was needed."

Night allowed his senses to sink into the awareness of having Zach close to him again. "And how did Uyla get into it all?"

"I told her that Kal came to me and said she wanted to see me. Then he took me to Orshan. When she questioned him, we found out that Kal was being used to gain Dominion Agva's vote."

"Tisus will take care of Orshan now, and I have the feeling we'll be addressing the matter of a new Dominion for his domain, Zach."

A smile twitched at Zach's lips, and his arm tightened around Night's waist before he released the vampire to step into their quarters. "You realize I never doubted I would find your domain. The odd thing was nobody tried to stop me in the first place."

Closing the door behind him, Night's gaze followed Zach as the young mortal moved toward the bed, stripping off his shirt. "Orshan wanted you to escape. It made it impossible for me to rescue you. And I don't believe he expected you to reach my castle.

"Weak mortal, I know." Zach rolled his eyes and sat on the bed, removing his shoes and pants.

"The Imperial command will deal with him now."

As Night stilled in front of him, Zach reached for him, wrapping his arms around Night's thighs. When their eyes met, both were aware of the barely suppressed emotions just beneath their casual conversation. Zach's voice lowered with husky undertone. "And you will deal with me now, Night."

"I think that we will be returning to my domain as soon as I can make the arrangements." As he spoke, Night unfastened his robe and slowly undressed. "No doubt Kat will be happy when we return home."

Zach stood, moving close to Night. He brushed Night's hands away and slipped the robe off his shoulders. "I want to go home, Night. I miss it, miss Kat…" He lowered his head and kissed Night's neck, near his shoulder. "Missed this…"

Night responded to the warmth of Zach's lips against skin. A soft growl rumbled from him as he shivered. Pulling back his head to look at Zach, Night said softly, "If you hadn't returned to me, I would have killed him without thought. From now on, you don't go anywhere without me until we leave here."

Zach looked like he was going to argue, but then he smiled. "All right. But only if you promise to be less of a stubborn mule."

"Do you really think I'm going to let you out of my sight for even a short time." His lips twitched into a smile, but there was a gleam of determined obstinacy in his eyes. Before Zach could get in another word, Night silenced him with a kiss. His lips covered Zach's then opened him to a hungry assault.

A soft gasp escaped Zach when Night released him. The heat of the vampire's gaze sent ripples of aching need through Zach, and without thought, he slid back onto the bed. On his hands and knees, the spread of his legs was a clear invitation to Night.

Another soft growl answered him before Night's edged in behind Zach. His hand cupped Zach's ass, smoothing over the flesh in a teasing touch. As his thumb inched along the crack of Zach's ass, Zach quickly reached for the nearby jar of salve. Both of them were caught in the moment.

After he took the jar from Zach, Night opened it

and dipped his fingers in the slippery substance. Resting his head on his forearm, Zach opened his legs further, waiting for that first touch. A soft moan sounded from him in impatience when only the feather light touch of Night's hand brushed the cheek of his ass.

The small noise suddenly took on a desperate edge when Zach felt slick fingers entering him. The sway of his body pushed back in an attempt to feel more. He heard Night's soft chuckle and gasped out. "More. Harder."

Night increased the teasing pressure, knuckles grazing Zach's prostate, making Zach jerk with the strengthening ache growing in him. Leaking steadily now, Zach grabbed at his cock. His hand bobbed frantically over the hard flesh, but he wanted a hell of a lot more.

In pure delight, Night took his time. He leaned against Zach's ass, his cock rubbing beneath him as his fingers plied inside Zach, slicking the walls. A ragged groan from Zach rewarded his efforts, and the urgent rock of Zach's hip pressed insistently against him. Unable to still his own need for their connection, Night finally pulled his hand away. With one motion, he burrowed inside Zach, sliding deeper and deeper until he'd settled fully in him.

Their bodies joined, Night's thoughts surrounded Zach's drawing the young mortal into him; body, mind, and soul. Small whimpers rose in Zach's throat as Night pulled him up and against him.

Night nuzzled against Zach's throat, claiming him fully as his fangs sank into the delicate skin. Zach shuddered against him in the throes of his own orgasm, and Night drank slowly from him, feeling the heated blood surge through his system. Enthralled by the soft cries and response of Zach's body, Night's own desire strengthened into a tight coil, leaving him senseless to the world as it exploded over him.

He ran his hand over Zach's chest, unleashing a small amount of his power as he continued drinking from Zach. Unable to control the urge, Night marked him, fully bonding Zach as his own. The transfer of energy sent a shock wave through Zach, and he leaned heavily against Night, both hands desperately gripping Night's hips.

A moment later, Zach collapsed to the bed, trying to catch his breath. Night moved to the bed, stretching beside him. His hand caressed soothingly along Zach's back, keeping the total connection between them.

"What did you do?" Zach gasped out, still reeling from the effects of what had happened.

"You are now completely mine in the ways of my people, Zach. Your status is equal to mine. If any try to harm you, they will be punished as if they had acted against me."

Shocked, Zach stared at him as he tried to find the words to say. He already understood what this was all about. If Orshan hadn't been guilty of trying to stack the petition vote in his favor, he would have never been severely punished for simply kidnapping a mortal. Finally, he said quietly, "You do love me."

"Yes." By nature, Night wasn't openly emotional, but for a brief moment, his expression softened, revealing the truth of his own feelings.

Zach twisted to his side, nudging against Night, mesmerized by the painful need apparent on Night's features. "As much I love you, I will never leave you, Night. I swear."